FLOWERS FOR THE JOURNEY

Thirty, Clare reflects on her birthday, is a milestone in her life. Despite being a successful lawyer with a comfortable lifestyle in Melbourne, she feels that she's in a rut, particularly in her relationship with Robert. She wonders whether she wants to remain in it forever. And then a surprising letter amongst her birthday cards prompts Clare to take a holiday to meet the person who penned it, and a man and a dog with the power to change her life. With the security she has earned, dare she choose this alternative future?

Books by Louise Pakeman
Published by The House of Ulverscroft:

THE PUMPKIN SHELL
CHANGE OF SKIES

Louise Pakeman was born in Cannock but has lived in Australia for the past thirty-eight years. Now retired, she has held a variety of jobs including work in publishing, as a freelance journalist and as a breeder of horses and donkeys.

LOUISE PAKEMAN

FLOWERS FOR THE JOURNEY

Complete and Unabridged

ULVERSCROFT
Leicester

First published in Great Britain in 2005 by
Robert Hale Limited
London

First Large Print Edition
published 2006
by arrangement with
Robert Hale Limited
London

British Library CIP Data

Pakeman, Louise, *1936 –*
    Flowers for the journey.—Large print ed.—
    Ulverscroft large print series: general fiction
    1. Woman lawyers—Australia—Fiction
    2. Large type books
    I. Title
    823.9′2 [F]

    ISBN 1–84617–329–9

Published by
F. A. Thorpe (Publishing)
Anstey, Leicestershire

Set by Words & Graphics Ltd.
Anstey, Leicestershire
Printed and bound in Great Britain by
T. J. International Ltd., Padstow, Cornwall

This book is printed on acid-free paper

1

Clare Davenport woke up on the morning of her thirtieth birthday with very mixed feelings. She felt good because she always enjoyed having a birthday, and today the sun was shining and it was a Friday, which meant it was the last day of the working week, but tempering her pleasure was the fact that she was thirty, a significant age in any woman's life. By leaving her twenties behind she was, she felt, leaving her youth — and thirty was a sharp reminder that her biological clock was ticking on, steadily and inexorably. She stretched out in bed, yawned and turned her mind to more positive thoughts.

Today, she told herself, was the first day of the rest of her life: time to take stock and to look at what she had done so far and where she was going. Most important of all, did she want to keep on in the same direction?

Where she had come from was easy enough, as was what she had done. As far as achievements went, she could say nil. She was not being quite fair to herself here: after all, she had graduated from law school and for the last several years had earned not only a good salary but a reputation as an up-and-coming divorce lawyer. The thing was that, as an incurable romantic deep down, being in the business of ending marriages did not satisfy her need to do something worthwhile with her life.

The big question was, did she want to go on into her thirties, maybe even her forties, just the same? There was, of course, Robert: good, kind, solid Robert who was very well established as partner in a more prestigious law firm than her own and who from time to time expressed a desire to marry her. There were two snags, however: the first that he already had a wife, the second that she wasn't at all sure that was what she wanted. Even as she thought this, it flashed into her mind with almost painful clarity that it wasn't. She switched her thoughts to her work life but quickly put them in the too-hard basket. One major decision was enough, even if — or maybe because — it was her birthday.

There was no gainsaying, however, that today was the first day of the rest of her life, and it was her life to make of it what she wanted. On that thought she leapt out of bed just as the phone rang.

'Robert! What a lovely surprise to hear you so early.' Habit made her slightly husky voice express pleasure when she heard his voice,

2

and anyway she was feeling good this morning because it was her birthday. Even turning thirty did not subdue her good spirits.

'Happy birthday, Clare.' Was it her imagination or did he sound — what? Cool, restrained. Of course not. Well, no more than usual; restraint was part of Robert's make-up.

'Wonderful to wake up to your voice,' Clare babbled, and cursed herself for sounding so uncoolly grateful, 'I mean . . . I didn't expect to hear from you till tonight.'

'Ah, well .. about tonight . . . ' Her ears caught the guilty note of apology in his voice. 'I'm just so sorry but I can't make it.'

'What do you mean, you can't make it?' Clare demanded, trying hard to keep the accusatory note out of her voice. She had kept this evening free for him. 'You promised!' she added, forgetting how Robert hated it when she showed any sign of possessiveness, however slight.

'I've said I'm sorry. But Linda has asked these people to dinner — it could be an important connection. I need to be there. In fact, I have to be there. After all, you and I can go out to dinner any night.'

But it won't be my birthday — This time Clare managed to keep the rather childish complaint where it belonged, inside her head.

3

'Of course,' she said diplomatically, feigning an air of coolness she was very far from feeling.

'Perhaps tomorrow. I'll call you.'

'No, not tomorrow. I can't make tomorrow.'

'Oh well — some other time. We must celebrate your birthday.'

'Of course,' Clare murmured dutifully. 'Actually, today would have been a dual celebration — two years.'

'Two years?'

Clare knew he had forgotten. 'The first time you took me out was two years ago, my twenty-eighth birthday,' she explained patiently. 'I had been stood up then, too.'

'But I haven't stood you up, Clare, just postponed our dinner. It would only have been for one day if you had been able to come tomorrow.'

He had managed, as he so often did, to turn the tables so that she was in the wrong. Well, it was her birthday, and she wasn't going to start it off by feeling guilty. Or let down, stood up or any other negative emotion.

'Thanks for ringing so early in the morning.' She hoped her cheerful voice would convince Robert that she didn't care that he had let her down. Yet again, she hadn't fooled herself. She replaced the phone with exaggerated care, crushing the desire to slam it down hard then scream and yell. Instead she stretched, yawned and made an effort to turn her mind to more positive thoughts. 'Today,' she told herself again, with as much optimism as she could muster at 7.15 in the morning, 'is the first day of the rest of my life.' *Yeah, more of the same ad infinitum. Time to take stock to look at what she had done so far, and where she was going. Most important of all, did she want to keep on in the same direction?* That was what the voice inside her was saying, and it was more insistent than the positive-thinking tape she was endeavouring to play to herself inside her head.

She hadn't expected turning thirty to be such a powerful thing. Up till now she had cruised along relatively satisfied with her life. For two years she had been quite happy with the arrangement she had with Robert. As a successful young lawyer with time on her side and no domestic aspirations, it suited her. After all, Robert could be a charming companion when he chose. But now the question — did she want to go on through her thirties, maybe even her forties, in the same old way — had arisen and she didn't know the answer. Robert would marry her if he was free, or would he? For the first time since she had known him, it crossed Clare's mind that he would probably not, and to her surprise, she didn't care.

Robert's firm was older and more established than hers — he dealt mostly in property transference — and Clare sometimes thought he considered what she did rather infra dig. He had not said so but it was just a feeling she got that he felt his work was more serious, more worthwhile, than hers. She had met him at a legal conference when she had discovered, to her dismay, that her promised lift home had left without her. He had stepped in, a true knight in shining armour, and given her a ride on his white charger, which in actual fact was a white Commodore. That had been the beginning. Out of courtesy she had invited him in for a drink and thought that was that. However, a week later she had bumped into him again and they had lunched together and from that had followed dinner and still later on, bed.

Young, unsure of herself and surprisingly inexperienced due to the necessity to keep her head down and work and her inner conviction that she was dull and unattractive, Clare had been flattered, then, when his skilful love-making awakened her, both grateful and in love with him. She had

6

convinced herself that she was a professional career woman, that marriage was not in her life plan, and so the fact that Robert was married and appeared to have no desire to get unmarried had seemed, if anything, fortuitous. Till now.

'Today is the first day of my life.' She repeated the words out loud this time and really meant them. She walked over to the window and threw back the curtains; it looked like being a beautiful day. 'And it is *my* life,' she added, still talking out loud to herself. 'It is up to me to make what I want of it.' On that salutary thought, she gathered up bra and panties and, humming softly to herself, headed for the shower.

'Happy birthday to you, happy birthday to you, happy birthday dear Clare . . . ', she sang to herself as she squeezed sweet-scented shower gel liberally over her wet skin. Rubbing shampoo vigorously into her scalp, she changed to, 'I'm going to wash that man right out of my hair . . . ', which she sang with more enthusiasm than finesse.

When she stepped out of the shower stall and wrapped herself in a thick bath sheet she felt about a hundred per cent better than she had when she stepped in. Back in fact to how she had felt when she first opened her eyes to her thirtieth birthday, before Robert's early-morning call made, she knew, while he did his duty lap of the block. Robert took his health seriously, so much so that Clare had once told him that she thought his motto was, 'I'll be healthy if it kills me.' He had not seen the joke and she had to explain it to him, by which time, of course, it was dead.

She filled the kettle at the sink for her caffeine fix, and had just dropped a second piece of bread into the toaster — a birthday indulgence, she usually limited herself to one — when she saw the postie moving away from the bank of mailboxes belonging to the small block of flats. She lived in the ground floor one, and because it was her birthday ran out in her dressing gown, something she had never done before, to collect her post. There was a satisfying little wad, bound together with an elastic band.

Perched on a stool, she ran through them as she munched on her toast and sipped her hot coffee. Five were birthday cards. Robert had not sent her a card but that neither surprised nor concerned her, like most of the men she knew he was not into choosing cards, and it was one of the chores he left to his wife. There were a couple more, one she knew was a bill, the other she suspected might be. She left both unopened on the

8

bench, while she arranged the cards on top of a small bookcase.

She was just leaving her flat when her mobile phone rang. She pulled it out of her pocket and answered it on her way out. It was Robert, again, calling from his car this time, to wish her a happy birthday again. At first she had been charmed and touched when he rang more than once to say the same thing, then it began to irritate her. She thanked him, yet again, then hung up with the excuse that she had to rush. She snapped off her phone and dropped it back in the pocket of her coat and decided to walk to her office, not take the bus as she had originally intended. It was only a few blocks and in good weather was much preferable to a crowded bus. City parking had become such a hassle, and so expensive, that she seldom took her car. This brief walk to start the day gave her a chance to think about any problems looming in the hours ahead She often thought of it as a sort of meditation time and came to resent any intrusions on it. There was no need at all to rush — she was in plenty of time so why had she told Robert she had to run and hung up on him so quickly?

She had almost reached her office before she gave herself the obvious answer. Because she didn't want to talk to him just then. She shied away from asking herself the obvious follow-up question,

'Happy birthday, Clare!'

'Many happy returns!' Naomi and Jodie chorused from behind the reception desk as she pushed open the heavy swing door of Macklin and Thomas, solicitors. Clare firmly repressed the familiar gripe about the brass plate: it was high time it was Macklin, Thomas and Davenport, she thought. But it was her birthday and she was not going to let anything, or anyone, stop her enjoying it.

'Gee, thanks, girls!' She smiled her appreciation as Naomi handed her two bright parcels and two envelopes. Behind her at the computer station Jodie grinned and gave the thumbs-up sign as she answered the telephone.

'Your first appointment is in half an hour,' Jodie called after her as she headed off down the corridor to her own office, where Zoe Keating was waiting for her with fresh coffee, the day's mail and a huge bunch of flowers. Not to mention a wide smile.

'Happy birthday! Thirty — just tipping over the hill. All down now to forty!'

Clare grinned back. 'You are totally insubordinate — I have no idea why I put up with you!'

'Course you do. You have known me too

long and you couldn't cope without me.'

'You're so right!' Clare meant to answer in the same light-hearted banter but looking at her lifelong friend, now her personal secretary, she knew how true it was. 'Who would have thought when we were both fifteen and planning out our lives that we would actually make it all happen and still be together all these years down the track?'

'You made it all happen; I had a few deviations along the way and didn't quite make it.' Zoe's smile was slightly rueful.

'I've heard kids called lots of things but never deviations before,' Clare laughed. 'You changed your life plan slightly and got married and had a couple of gorgeous kids, that's all.'

'You sound quite maudlin, Clare. You're not feeling you've missed out, surely? You have achieved your goal: here you are, the hot-shot lawyer, successful and dedicated career woman, with a lover, but no ties and no strings attached.'

'Did I really say that was what I wanted?' Clare looked thoughtful as she went back to those heady college days when their lives and the future lay before them. 'Yes, I probably did. It was what I imagined would be the ideal life in those days. So, for a time, did you.'

'Yeah, but I stuffed it up, didn't I? Got pregnant, got married, gave up law — in that order.' Suddenly brisk, Zoe turned away and thrust the huge bunch of flowers at Clare. 'Happy birthday, from Robert,' she read on the card. Certainly nothing flowery in his wording. She turned away from the amused glint in Zoe's eye and headed for the washroom.

'I'll stick these in the sink: I'm sure we haven't got a vase big enough for them. What the hell did he have to send them here for, anyway?'

'I guess he has to apologize . . . '

'Apologize? What do you mean?'

'Men always send flowers when they feel guilty about something. Surely you know that, Clare.'

'Well, yes. He cancelled our dinner date.'

Zoe shrugged. 'There you are . . . '

Clare didn't wait to hear any more; she put the flowers in the washroom sink in cold water and returned to the office. 'I guess we had better get some work done — I can't sit around just because it happens to be my birthday.'

It was not so easy to settle down to the nuts and bolts of everyday work. Clare found her thoughts wandering in strange byways. Curiously, it was Zoe pointing out that she had got where she wanted to be that made her question her life. She had always said, and truly believed, that she was perfectly happy, and had often said, only half jokingly, that her job as a divorce lawyer ensured that she never wasted time and energy yearning after marriage. Now, for the first time, she wondered.

'Do you ever regret it, Zoe?' she asked suddenly in the middle of dictating a letter.

'Regret it? What?'

'Getting married — not sticking with the dream.'

'But I did. Just didn't achieve it all. My dream was to be a hot-shot lawyer and have a husband and kids. I just had to settle for half, that's all, and you settled for the other half.'

'Yeah, I suppose so.' Clare had never considered that that was what she had done. Now she wasn't at all sure. They were both thirty now: Zoe had two kids growing up fast, while she had a beautiful but sterile home and a love affair that had gone on too long and was now, she felt, dangerously near its 'use by' date.

* * *

The first thing she noticed when she let herself into her flat were the two envelopes

13

she had dismissed earlier on as bills. One was a gas bill, of all mundane things to receive on one's birthday. Then she opened the other and when she drew out the single sheet of paper and saw the office heading of a firm of solicitors she almost threw it down in irritation. Her first thought was that it must be a letter that had somehow got sent to her personal address when it should have gone to her office. But because she was a compulsive reader, unable to cast anything with the printed word on to one side, she began to read.

She read it through several times before the full gist of the letter became clear, not because the legal phraseology made it difficult, but because, even though it was clearly addressed to her, the content seemed to have no relevance for her.

'Dear Miss Davenport,' she read half aloud to herself. 'Would you please contact me with reference to the estate of your aunt, the late Hester McMaster.' The letter heading was that of a firm of solicitors in Castlemaine and the name at the bottom was one Timothy Trimble, who appeared to be a partner in the firm. It was all very official and businesslike, the only thing was she had not got an aunt, alive or dead, called Hester McMaster. In fact she had no one. Not in Australia, anyway.

Since her father's death nearly three years ago she had been quite alone. Or had she? Somewhere in the deep recesses of her memory there was a dim idea that both parents had once taken her, in the days before they parted, to see a very old aunt of her father. She had a vague memory of her mother dressing her up in her best clothes and abjuring her to be on her best behaviour because this aunt was rich. She seemed to recall this remark of her mother's had annoyed her father and triggered off one of their many rows.

So maybe there was a connection after all. Shortly after that, Dad had left for England and she had lived with her mother and a succession of 'uncles' for the next few years. Now it seemed this aunt was dead and she, Clare Davenport, was being summoned to her lawyer's office. She glanced at her watch. It was pretty late on a Friday afternoon but she dialled the number on the off chance that this Timothy Trimble might still be in his office.

She was about to put the phone down on the assumption he was not when it was answered by a somewhat brusque male voice bristling with impatience. She sympathized: clients who rang at the very end of the week were a bugbear.

'Ah, Miss Davenport, I am so glad I managed to track you down and you have contacted me. It is about your aunt, Miss Hester McMaster, who, I am sorry to say, died recently.'

'Yes.' Clare tried to keep the impatience out of her voice; he had told her all this in his letter.

'Now it seems that as her only relative you stand to inherit the greater part of her estate.'

'But I didn't know her!' Clare protested. 'Barely even knew she existed.'

'Yes, well, be that as it may, she has left you the bulk of her estate. However, there are one or two, well, clauses, conditions — so I would very much appreciate it if you could manage to come to Castlemaine and see me.'

'But — ' Clare began to protest.

If he heard, he took no notice, 'If you could let me know which day next week is suitable for you?'

'Are you available Saturday morning?'

'I can be, certainly,' came the suave reply.

'Then I will be up next weekend.'

'You couldn't make it tomorrow?'

Clare was about to say yes but a quick mental review of her workload over the next week made her repeat that it was impossible. She had some holiday due and if she got things up to date she could take a few days,

16

maybe even a week, and give herself a break. It would be a birthday treat to herself.

'I am sorry, I'm too busy. But I will definitely be there the following week.' As she replaced the receiver it struck her as sad that the old lady had died without anybody she knew and cared about to leave her property to. She must have been very much alone if her lawyers had to search out such a distant connection as herself. She was so busy thinking sympathetic thoughts about this unknown relative that it didn't cross her mind that she should have made an appointment.

By the time she took herself to bed with a good book and a hot drink, the staid replacement for the birthday dinner with Robert, Clare had decided that if the old lady had left her a few bucks she would treat herself to a really good overseas holiday.

She debated whether or not to call Robert and tell him about the letter but his cancelling of the birthday dinner still rankled. She reflected, somewhat sourly, that it wouldn't hurt him if she was unavailable for a whole week.

*   *   *

A couple of days later, when Clare's car refused to start, because she had left a door not quite shut and the interior light had run the battery down, she did what had become a habit in such circumstance — called Robert and asked him to come round with his jump leads. When he suggested dinner that night she accepted; it seemed churlish to refuse when he had just come to her rescue.

'Just instruct the lawyers to sell up whatever property she has and send you the money,' Robert advised, when she told him all about the legacy over the dinner table.

'I don't like to do that, it seems — oh, I don't know, sort of a bit cold and heartless somehow,' Clare demurred.

'Don't be silly, Clare, you never met the woman. In fact, you had a hard job to work out who she was. Just do the sensible thing — tidy everything up and collect.'

Clare studied him across the dinner table in the expensive, dimly lit restaurant he had chosen to take her to for this belated birthday dinner. He had turned his attention to the menu and was studying it with total concentration, lips pursed, brows drawn together in a faint frown of concentration. Clare didn't care much what they ate; she wanted to talk. 'Oh, you choose for me.' She put the large folded menu down with a firm slap on the table.

'I thought the sirloin — they do beef well

18

here. And a good red to go with it.'

Clare thought his choice dull, but having asked him to choose she accepted it. It struck her that Robert was somewhat dull too. Or maybe it was just familiarity; even illicit relationships could fall into a rut if maintained for too long. Had theirs become no more than a habit?

'I shall go and see these lawyers and find out just what I have inherited,' she announced as he put down his copy of the menu and looked round for the waiter.

'That is absurd; you can do all you need to do from here.' It was gratifying to see she had his attention, anyway.

'I could do with a break — in fact, I am due for some holiday. I shall put in for it,' Clare went on, ignoring his comment as if he had never made it. Just saying it out loud strengthened her determination. It was true — she was due for holidays and she needed a break, from Robert as much as anything. The thought surprised her but did nothing to change her mind; quite the contrary, in fact.

'I thought you said the lawyer was in Castlemaine?'

Clare nodded and smiled up at the waiter as he placed her order in front of her.

'No need to stay, then. You can just go for the day. I could come with you.'

'I shall take a week, I think . . . ' Clare spoke distantly from some isolated space in her head. 'I've only passed through the town on my way to somewhere else before. A holiday there exploring the area would be pleasant.'

'If you want to go for a holiday, why not go somewhere decent?'

'Do you know Castlemaine well?'

'Never been there,' Robert snorted.

'Ah, well, then, you don't really know whether it is worth staying in or not, do you?' Clare asked with sweet reasonableness. 'If I find it very dull then I will head off somewhere else. I really do need a break, and this has given me a reason to go somewhere . . . ' She let her voice trail off with a vague smile and a slight shrug. Robert knew her well enough to know that this air of vagueness covered an implacable will and that she had made her mind up and would not be moved. He began to talk about something else.

When Robert glanced openly at his watch, Clare knew he had given his wife a time that he would return. 'Where are you tonight?' she asked with some asperity.

He didn't pretend to misunderstand. 'At a Rotary dinner.' He looked at his watch again. 'While you finish your coffee, I'll make a phone call — '

'Don't bother — you'll be home in good time. I'd really rather you didn't come in tonight.' Clare, sipping her coffee with maddening slowness, looked at Robert across the table with a dispassionate eye. Could it really have taken her two years to see him for what he was: a dull, pompous man, just hitting middle age yet still playing this absurd 'spy thriller' game with himself. Clare found it hard to believe that Linda did not have a good idea what was going on. Surely it was not possible that he could have fooled her for so long with his lies and subterfuges, such as ringing from a public call box so that she wouldn't know just where he was? No doubt she pretended to be taken in because it suited her own agenda, whatever that was, Clare thought with some cynicism.

'I'm tired, and I want to go home for a reasonably early night . . . ' Clare began, then paused while she thought how best to tell him that she didn't really want to see him again. 'I think perhaps you and I have come to the end of the road . . . Our relationship has gone about as far as it can — ' She faltered and he cut in quickly.

'You *are* tired, so don't say any more right now; something you may regret later on. You know my position. I've always been honest with you. I always said there was no way I could walk out of my marriage while Annabel was young. When she is older — '

'Some time in the never-never,' Clare retorted dryly. Robert looked at her, surprised; she had never been difficult about things before. He thought maybe it was her job: she no doubt heard so much about the perfidy between men and women and the mess they made of their relationships it was making her cynical. Busy with his own musings, he was taken by surprise when she added, 'As for honesty — you don't know the meaning of the word, Robert. You've cheated on Linda and you've cheated on me. Worst of all, you have told yourself your precious sanctimonious lies so long that now you believe them.' She bent to retrieve her handbag from the floor, pushed back her chair and stood up.

'Clare!' Seeing the blank amazement on his face, Clare almost laughed out loud. 'Where are you going? Wait — I have to settle the bill.'

'Home — by taxi — alone.' Good manners forced her to add, 'Thanks for the dinner.'

With remarkably fortuitous timing, a taxi was just drawing up at the kerb to discharge a couple of late diners, and she was in and driving away while Robert was still settling the bill. She wanted to laugh out loud but, not wanting to appear drunk, she managed to tone it down to a suppressed giggle. Drunk or not, she felt quite lightheaded as she thought of Robert's expression, and once inside her own apartment she poured herself a glass of wine and stood in front of the mirror. She raised her glass to herself and freedom.

★ ★ ★

'So . . . ' she said to Zoe next morning after she had given her a quick run-through of what she had said to Robert the previous evening. 'That's it — fob him off, cut him off, do what you like if he rings me, but don't put him through.'

'Are you afraid you might weaken?'

'No, I don't think I would, but two years is quite a while. He's become a sort of habit.'

'One you should have broken long ago — or never even started,' Zoe told her. 'There is no future in married men, unless of course you are married to them. Being the other woman is lousy.'

'Yeah — I'm forced to admit you are right.'

'Better late than never — I told you, there is nothing romantic about it — men are such arseholes, they want the bun and the penny.'

'No one would think you were happily married.'

23

'I'm happily married because I'm a realist, not a romantic,' Zoe retorted, 'and Brendan knows that if he messed around I'd be out — or he would!'

'Do you think I'm a romantic?' Clare was surprised at this assessment of herself.

''Course you are — you saw yourself as the love of his life and vice versa, and you imagined you would have all the roses and none of the thorns. Time to grow up, Clare — give yourself a break and forget him.'

'That is just what I intend to do,' Clare said firmly, and quickly outlined the letter she had received from the Castlemaine lawyer and her plans. 'So, we'd better get some work done so that I can leave things ship-shape here,' she finished.

They had hit a tolerably slack time; it seemed not too many people wanted to get out of their marriages at the moment and Clare was able to arrange her work so that she could have the next week off. She headed out of Melbourne on Friday evening for the Midlands town of Castlemaine, some two hours' drive. Or it should have been, and would have been, had half of Melbourne not got the same idea. As she fumed in the packed traffic, all heading out of the city at a snail's pace, Clare thanked herself for the forethought that had made her book a motel as soon as she had decided to go.

She had not thought to check the lawyer's office would be open on Saturday morning, however, and found it closed. Oh, well, she would spend the weekend doing what she had promised herself anyway — exploring the area.

She spent Saturday in Castlemaine wandering round on foot, charmed by the old buildings and discovering several pleasant eating places. On Sunday she chose to go further afield and after studying the various leaflets and brochures headed out for Maldon.

She found an incredibly busy small town, little more than a village, in fact, but almost every shop seemed to be open, full of customers and selling mostly touristy things. The only exceptions to this were the everyday businesses. She had the feeling that she was in a film set rather than an actual place. However, the goods for sale were very real and she set out to enjoy browsing. As books were her great weakness, she spent a lot of time in the bookshop, lingered over a lunch in a pleasant café and then continued her exploration.

At the top end of the main street was a florist's shop, but it was closed. This surprised Clare: she would have expected it to fall into the category of those shops likely to appeal to the tourist, rather than the more mundane shops that were closed at weekends. She had amused herself as she walked down the street, reading the hours of business, and had come to the conclusion there were two Maldons, as far as shopping was concerned. There were those that opened in the week to supply the day-to-day needs for the local people, and the ones that only opened on weekends and holidays to serve the influx of tourists.

She stopped now in front of the florist, the name painted a long time ago judging by its tired and faded look. In an arc across the window, it read 'Flowers For The Journey'. It struck her as being an odd name, and somewhat ambiguous. She peered through the windows. They could do with a clean, she thought, and saw a few bunches of flowers standing in buckets, limply sending out the message to the world that they were very near, if they hadn't actually reached, their 'Best Before' date. To one side were some insipid-looking potted palms. The only splash of colour was offered by a stack of flowering cyclamens standing by a small chalk board on which was scrawled the legend 'Half Price.'

Clare amused herself for a short while, standing in front of this depressing run-down shop which stuck out like a sore thumb amidst the almost frenetic activity of the other businesses dedicated to extracting dollars from tourists. There was a rather faded hand-written notice on the door, which Clare, being a compulsive reader, moved closer to decipher. 'Part-time help wanted', she read in some surprise. It didn't look to her as if it was likely to do enough business to keep its present workforce occupied.

★   ★   ★

The following morning Clare faced the lawyer across the wide expanse of oak desk in an office that could have come straight out of a film set; either that, she thought, or nothing had been changed in it for the last fifty years. Nothing, that is, except the lawyer himself. She guessed he had not yet passed forty, so he had to be of a younger vintage than his surroundings and could not have been behind that impressive desk for fifty years.

'Ah, come in, Miss . . er . . . Miss Davenport.' He smiled at her rather vaguely and indicated the chair on her side of the desk. 'Do sit down, please.'

Clare sat, and resisted the temptation to tell him that she preferred Ms to Miss. It had a ring of independence totally lacking in the formal old-fashioned Miss. She folded her hands in her lap and waited, surprising herself by enjoying the sensation of being the client rather than the lawyer.

'Er . . . Miss . . . er . . . Davenport, you . . . er . . . received our letter?'

'That's why I'm here, Mr Er . . . ?' Clare had genuinely forgotten the name on the bottom of the letter she had received from the firm of Knight, Boyd and Trimble, but by the rather startled glance he threw at her she guessed that he was wondering if she meant to be facetiously humorous. 'I'm sorry — I don't think I caught your name,' she mumbled apologetically.

He smiled, and she realized he was probably only a few years older than herself, and really quite attractive. 'Trimble, I'm Timothy Trimble,' he told her.

'And I'm Clare Davenport. Can we drop that austere Miss, please?'

He smiled again. Yes, he was definitely attractive, Clare thought.

'Well, Clare Davenport, it would seem you are the only surviving relative of Hester McMaster and as such inherit her entire estate.' Timothy Trimble paused to let this momentous news sink in.

'Which amounts to?' She had felt compelled to say something to fill in the silence and now wished she had kept quiet; it sounded such a mercenary question.

'Her house, her business and . . . ' he consulted the sheaf of papers in the folder tied with the ubiquitous pink lawyer's tape. 'Her jewellery and . . . ' He paused again and seemed to be having difficulty controlling his amusement at some secret joke. 'And her dog.'

'Her dog?' Clare repeated blankly. This interview was, she felt, getting quite surreal. 'Are you joking, Mr Trimble?'

'I can assure you this is no joke, Miss . . . er . . . Davenport.'

'Call me Clare,' she snapped. If he said Miss . . . er . . . Davenport once again she was sure she would scream.

'It is no joke at all, Clare,' he repeated, but she thought he looked as if he found it very amusing, for all his protestations.

'Then please explain.'

'Everything is left to you — everything — on condition that you look after her dog.'

'But I can't — I live in a flat. You know what rental properties are like — no pets allowed. Anyway, I am at work all the time. I couldn't look after him properly . . . '

He held his hand up in a silencing gesture and her words trailed away to hang in the silence between them. 'I'm afraid you haven't heard the terms of her will yet. Taking him to live with you isn't an option.'

'What do you mean? I suppose if I have to I can take him to my flat. What sort of a dog is he, by the way? A Yorkie, a miniature poodle?' she asked hopefully. Maybe she could smuggle something that size into her life.

Timothy Trimble grinned, and Clare got the distinct impression he was enjoying himself. 'Not exactly. Boris is a Borzoi.'

'A Borzoi?' Clare frantically racked her brain to think what sort of dog that was. 'You don't mean a — a Russian wolfhound?' she asked faintly.

'That's right. Magnificent dogs. Boris is so large that when I went to see Miss McMaster once he jumped up and stood just about eyeball to eyeball with me — his paws on my shoulder. I'm five foot nine.'

'Well, obviously there is no way Boris can live with me,' Clare stated flatly.

Timothy Trimble looked at her in silence across that expanse of desk, a reflective and most irritating half-smile playing round the corners of his lips, which were, Clare noticed, full and shaped in a classic cupid's bow. 'No,' he agreed, 'you will have to live with him. He has a big house — and that is the terms of the will, anyway.'

Clare stared at him. It seemed to her that the man was talking absolute gibberish, unless he was joking, so she decided to ignore what he had said. 'I am afraid you will have to make some arrangements for the dog. I shall, of course, sell the property. Maybe you could arrange that for me,' She had risen to her feet as she spoke.

'Please sit down Miss . . . er . . . Clare. You have not understood. You cannot sell the property; your inheriting it is contingent upon you taking care of Boris. And as you cannot have him to live with you then you have no alternative but to live with him. This, of course, is what Miss McMaster wanted — she was anxious that Boris should not be uprooted from his home after her death. To that end she really wanted to leave everything to him. I talked her out of that, but only by suggesting the alternative that I have just outlined to you.'

Clare sat down heavily in the chair she had just vacated. 'I . . . see . . . ' she murmured vaguely. She had never felt so confused in her life. 'And if I don't inherit — then what happens?'

'Ah well, should you decline to accept the terms then there are other contingents . . . '

His voice trailed off, but Clare wasn't having that. In her best clipped legal tones, she said, 'I presume these contingents are other possible heirs?'

Timothy nodded. 'Quite so, Miss . . . er . . . Davenport — er . . . Clare. I think I should be frank with you.' Clare nodded but didn't say anything. 'I was not very happy with your aunt's will; in fact, I did my best to make her change it.'

'Why?'

'I felt that — well I felt that there were more deserving people she could choose.' Clare felt a flash of annoyance that he didn't think her deserving. 'But she was adamant — you were her only blood relation.'

'Is this more deserving person likely to contest the will?' Even as she asked the question, Clare could hear Robert's voice in her head saying it.

'I doubt it.' A spasm of irritation crossed his face. 'Mark Fisk is far too much of an idealist. I mentioned to him once that I thought maybe he should have been the one remembered, but he brushed it aside, saying Hester McMaster had done more than enough for him when she was alive and anything she had should go to her blood relative — you.'

'Hmm.' In Clare's experience such quixotic nobility did not exist. Whatever he said, she could foresee trouble. 'And where is this

Mark Fisk now?' she asked.

'Oh, he is in Maldon, caretaking her house and managing her business, and — of course — looking after Boris.' He added the last with a slight smile.

'What is the business?' Clare asked, more out of idle curiosity than anything else.

'I'm afraid it is not in a good state — Hester let things go downhill very badly when she became sick . . . ' He paused. 'So sad — she was such a good businesswoman at one time. Still . . . '

'What is the business?' Clare asked again.

'Oh, didn't I tell you? It is a shop, a florist shop. Flowers For The Journey.'

2

Wouldn't you know it? Clare thought. First a house that is apparently owned by a dog and now that seedy little shop. This legacy was not worth having.

She rose to her feet slowly. 'I'll let you know what I intend to do,' she said aloud, thinking to herself, I don't want any part of this damn legacy. 'I need to think about it, but if those are the terms I really don't see how I can possibly accept — no doubt this Fisk person will be pleased to hear.'

'I don't think so. I thought I made that clear. He feels that Hester did so much for him while she was alive that he could not possibly take anything more.'

'How quixotic.' Clare's voice was dry. She didn't believe it.

'Think about it — please. Don't do anything rash. You are, after all, the person Hester chose to leave her estate to.'

Heading back for her motel, Clare thought that the rash thing would be to accept this crazy legacy with all its problems. All the same, it might not be a bad idea to have a look at Flowers For The Journey when it was

34

open and doing business, if it was. She turned the car away from her motel and headed out to Maldon.

It did look marginally brighter this morning now it was open. A man about her own age was serving a customer with one of the half-price cyclamens. Clare went inside and looked round, and was startled when he demanded in a voice that hardly sounded like a customer-wooing voice, 'If you've come about the job, I must tell you . . . ' When she thought about it afterwards, that was the moment she decided to take the job. What better way to find out what condition this run-down looking business was really in? 'Actually . . . ' she interrupted, pointlessly, for he went on to say, 'I must tell you it is only likely to be temporary. Pay is low and I can really only offer you a few hours each day.'

'How temporary?' Clare found herself asking.

'Depends. The owner has died; it has been left to some woman from Melbourne. I can't imagine she will want anything to do with it.'

'Can't you?' Clare asked. 'Why not?'

He shrugged and looked her up and down with the most amazing bright blue eyes Clare had ever seen, but she didn't care for his scrutiny any more than she liked his casual dismissal of her as 'some woman from

Melbourne'. 'Well, look at it. Would anyone in their right mind want to keep this on?'

Clare turned away from him; there was something about him, in addition to those incredible eyes, that disturbed her. She wasn't sure she liked him. She looked round the shop, giving it her full and, as much as possible, unbiased attention. It was true: it was run-down, untidy, utterly depressing, in fact, and yet something about it touched a dormant chord in her, almost as if it was a living, breathing entity. Something within her wanted to take it to heart, to murmur soothing platitudes; *Come along, dear, pull yourself together . . . We'll have you right in no time.* Was she going out of her mind?

She turned and looked straight into those azure eyes, then deliberately she let her gaze rove over the rest of him, much as he had done to her. 'It just looks thoroughly neglected to me, and that can always be remedied.' She spoke sharply, repressing a smile of satisfaction when she saw that her words had found their mark, 'I'll take the job,' she told him, 'but only for a week.'

'I haven't offered it to you,' he reminded her, 'but as you are willing, and you're the only person who seems to be, I might as well take you on, I suppose.' It was said grudgingly without any enthusiasm, but Clare

36

found herself flushing as his eyes took in her smartly casual clothes. 'You can hardly work in those.'

Clare shrugged, trying to find words to explain that she was unable to change into any less good clothes; what she had back at the motel were only more of the same. They stood and looked at one another for a moment then he said, grudgingly, 'There are some overalls in the back room. At least you can cover up.' He nodded towards a door at the back of the shop and, feeling about six years old, Clare obediently walked towards it. 'Hanging on the back of the door,' he called after her. 'By the way, my name's Mark. What's yours?'

'Clare,' she threw back over her shoulder as she pushed the door open to the chaotic nether regions of the shop. She found several green coat overalls on the single hook on the other side of the door. She pulled them down, one at a time, and studied them with a critical eye, selecting the one that seemed the cleanest, or, to be strictly accurate, the least dirty. It was all-enveloping — a nice way of saying much too big — but she put it on and walked back into the shop feeling absurdly self-conscious as she faced Mark.

It was the cleanest,' she told him defensively, noting the glint of amusement in his eyes before he turned away.

'Well, at least it covers you up.' They stood and looked at one another in an uncomfortable silence. Clare wondered how she was going to work with, or for, this man. From the expression on his face he was thinking much the same thing. 'What are you standing there for? You said it was easy enough to remedy the neglected look — let's see you do it.'

Clare opened her mouth to protest at what she felt was his insufferable rudeness, then shut it again as the bell attached to the door jangled and a somewhat dowdy middle-aged woman came in. Like the previous customer, she wanted one of the half-price cyclamens but took as long selecting one as if she were spending a hundred dollars. Clare saw a broom propped against the far wall and walked over to collect it and do something about straightening the place up. She soon had a pile of dirt, twigs and leaves and looked round for something to scoop them up with. She found a dustpan and brush in the back room and while there investigated a galvanized garbage bin full of dead flowers and leaves and stalk trimmings, obviously a suitable receptacle for her load of rubbish.

By the time the customer left with her cyclamen — still unsure, from the expression

on her face, that she had selected the best one
— Clare had swept the floor, tidied up a collection of pots and was ruefully surveying the few buckets containing rather tired-looking cut flowers. 'What do I do with these?' she asked Mark's back.

'Isn't it obvious?' he snapped, half turning towards her.

Clare pressed her lips together; she did not intend to let this incredibly rude man goad her into a response that would give him the excuse to get rid of her. She had taken this job on to help her decide whether this business was worth saving.

'Throw the dead ones away and re-bunch the rest in fresh water,' he told her as the bell clanged again and another customer, this time a man, walked up to the counter.

By the time she had finished with the flowers, the shop was empty once more. She surveyed the considerably reduced collection of buckets containing cut flowers and tried to arrange them so that they didn't look so sparse, wishing at the same time that she was a bit more up on flowers. The lilies she knew, of course, and the carnations, but some of the others . . .

'Do you know how to work the cash register, take credit cards?'

He sounded so doubtful that Clare was

stung into snapping back, 'Yes — I can answer a phone too!'

Briefly he looked startled. 'Good — you can take charge, then, for a while. I'm going to have lunch.'

Clare stared at his retreating back in amazement. No wonder the business wasn't doing well — correction, was doing badly. She toyed with the rather pleasing notion of giving Mark the sack once she took over. Then she had to pull her thoughts into line. Hold on, she admonished herself. Who said anything about that? I've already looked at the feasibility of accepting this legacy with all its ramifications. It's just not on. Yet in spite of her self-admonitions, she found herself looking round the shop with the keen eye of a prospective owner, and had tentatively opened a couple of drawers looking for financial records when the old-fashioned bell clanged again. It was the dowdy woman who had taken so long choosing her plant earlier on. Clare noticed she had it with her now.

'I'm sorry,' she said, not sounding it, 'but I'd like to change this for a different colour. I was getting it for a friend, you see. I had forgotten she quite detests white flowers — says they remind her of weddings, which are always so sad because they never turn out as people expect them to.' She exchanged the

40

white cyclamen for a vivid red as she spoke. 'Don't you find that? I think this will do, yes. I'll have this one, thanks. There's no charge — I just changed it,' she reminded Clare sharply, seeing her move towards the old-fashioned-looking cash register.

'I realize that,' Clare managed through gritted teeth, reminding herself that 'the customer is always right'.

As there were no more customers, she continued her tidying and rearranging. She had been tempted to tell the woman that as her job was untying the marriage knot, she saw weddings as the prospect of more business. But she kept her mouth firmly shut and instead wondered if Flowers For The Journey did much business supplying wedding flowers. Looking round the shop, she guessed not. Well, here's another opportunity, she thought.

In the hour that Mark left her in sole charge while he fortified the inner man, she sold one more half-price cyclamen, kept a weather-eye on a young couple briefly browsing but not buying and managed to sweep, tidy and partially rearrange to her own satisfaction. She was outside cleaning the window when Mark got back. He stopped on the pavement and watched her for a moment.

'What happens if a customer comes?'

41

'I go inside and serve them.' Clare bridled at what she felt was totally unwarranted criticism and fought back a childish urge to throw her bucket of water at him. She contented herself with adding, '*If* a customer comes.'

With something like a sniff or a grunt he went inside the shop. Clare continued to remove what she thought must be the dust and grime of years from the plate-glass window.

Bucket still in hand, she stepped back, straight into a strong, unyielding male body. Water from her bucket sloshed out over a shiny black lace-up business shoe as well as her own feet.

'Whoops!' The voice sounded apologetic and confused — and familiar. She turned to face its owner. 'Good heavens! Miss . . . er . . . Davenport . . . Clare!'

'Mr Trimble!' Clare thought she said, but though she knew her mouth had opened she could not hear her voice saying anything.

Simultaneously they each took a step back. Just as she had been when she first met him, Clare was surprised to see that he was only a few years older than herself. The name Trimble, especially in the setting of his office, conjured up an elderly, almost Dickensian character. Aware that, absurdly, she was

42

flushing, Clare dropped her eyes from his face. He continued his scrutiny of her and if Clare had still been looking at him she might have seen the amusement glinting in his eyes.

'Miss er . . . Davenport — Clare — could you tell me what you are doing in that . . . er . . . garment?'

Clare looked down at the grubby green overall enveloping her and felt her flush deepen to a blush. She tried vainly for insouciance. 'This — oh, I just put it on while I was cleaning up.'

'But why are *you* cleaning up?'

Clare stared at him helplessly. 'It needed doing,' she answered shortly. 'The windows were so filthy you couldn't see through them.'

'But why are *you* doing it?' he persisted.

Clare stared blankly back, thinking he must be good in court because he simply didn't let go. Finally she capitulated with a sigh. 'I work here,' she admitted.

'Aah . . . Well, I was just coming to tell Mark that we had located the heir to the property.' He made a move towards the door and Clare, without thinking, reached out and grabbed his arm.

'No — no, please don't. Let me explain,' she begged.

'Have you had lunch?'

'No . . . but . . . '

'Go in and say that you are taking a lunch break. I'll stay out here and hope I haven't been seen. I'll walk down to the milk bar.'

Obediently, Clare picked up her window-cleaning gear and returned to the shop. Mark was not visible. Unfastening her overall, she went through into the back room and found him poring over a pile of invoices — at least, that's what they looked like.

'I'm taking a lunch break,' she announced as confidently as she could. 'I've finished the window.' She wondered if he had heard and repeated her intention.

'I heard.' He didn't bother to look up from his task. Clare hung the overall back on the hook she had found it on, wondering if he was going to refuse her and gathering up in her head her arguments about workers' rights, but he remained silent.

Timothy Trimble was nowhere to be seen so she headed for the milk bar just down the road. It was not, she thought, as she pushed open the door and looked around, strictly a milk bar, much more a tearoom, as befitted Maldon. He was seated at a table for two in the far corner. Briefly she wondered why he had chosen that table and not one in the window where he could see her coming.

'Now,' he demanded when they had ordered coffee and toasted sandwiches, 'perhaps you can explain what on earth you were doing wearing fancy dress and cleaning windows?'

'It was not fancy dress — it was one of the shop overalls,' Clare explained. 'and I was cleaning the window because it was dirty.'

'But why were *you* doing it?'

'Because ... ' Suddenly the simple truth sounded incredibly stupid. She squirmed on her seat and smiled gratefully at the waitress who came at that moment with two cups of steaming, frothy cappuccino. She waited till the sandwiches had also arrived, then with a sigh began her explanation. 'I went to have a look at the business — just to see what it was like — and there was a notice up, 'Help wanted', so — '

'You applied for the job, thinking you would get an inside look and really know whether it was worthwhile accepting the challenge that your legacy was throwing at you?' Detecting an edge to his voice, Clare looked up, but his expression was bland.

'Something like that,' she mumbled.

'And what is your opinion?'

'As I've only been there an hour or so I have hardly had time to form one, but I have to say that from what I've seen so far it doesn't look a good option.'

'But someone of your intelligence and

ability could undoubtedly turn it round, if you wanted to.'

'But that's the point — do I want to?' She bit hungrily into her sandwich, savouring the hot cheese and tomato filling. 'How do you know I'm intelligent and able, anyway?' She looked up with a smile and found him watching her with a curious intensity which softened as she met his gaze. His face broke into a smile, making him look much younger.

'It takes ability and intelligence to get where you are.'

'Sitting here eating a sandwich and drinking coffee?'

'I know what you really do, Clare. You work for a prestigious law firm in Melbourne and you specialize in divorce.'

Clare wondered how he knew this but was not going to give him the satisfaction of asking. She swallowed a large piece of sandwich and smiled enigmatically. 'I guess,' she said, after a pause, 'that it takes one to know one — lawyer, I mean.'

'But does your . . . er . . . holiday job mean that you are rethinking your decision not to accept your inheritance?'

Clare chewed thoughtfully for a moment. 'I don't really know. I took that job on impulse; thought it would be a good way to find out what sort of a business it really was. I haven't really given it much thought beyond that.'

'Maybe you should. After all, if you didn't want to have anything to do with it, you could ask Mark to stay on as manager. It doesn't have to be a hands-on thing.'

'You mean I don't have to live in the shop?' Clare spoke ironically, thinking of the dog. It was all lost on Timothy, who, it appeared, was a trifle low on humour.

'Of course not. There is no living accommodation.'

'Look — I took this job impulsively, out of idle curiosity, nothing more. I might as well know what I am giving up. From what I have seen so far, this business would be as much or more of a liability than the dog, which seems to be a bar to my accepting anyway.'

'You could commute.'

'I could — theoretically — but spending half my time on a train hurtling between two points is not my idea of living.'

Timothy raised his eyebrows slightly. 'You could live the good life up here,' was all he said.

Clare was about to say she didn't need to move up here to do that, then, thinking of her life in Melbourne, her small flat, her unsatisfactory love life and her job which was just that, a job, she remained silent and sipped her coffee thoughtfully. 'I would like to have a look at the house. I suppose I can do that without committing myself?'

'But of course. Arrange it with Mark.'

'With Mark? But I — '

'He is living there at the moment.'

Clare stared at Timothy across the small table. 'You have to be joking.'

He shook his head. 'Why do you say that?'

Clare shrugged. 'I should have thought that as he is running the business, living in the house and looking after the dog, he wouldn't want to hand them over to a stranger.'

'I thought I had explained that to you. If you don't understand, maybe you should ask Mark himself.'

'Maybe I should.' But would she? There was something about the man that kept intimacy at bay. She had a feeling he would not welcome being interrogated on his reasons for not wanting what, from his position, must be a pleasant inheritance. If she didn't live and work in Melbourne . . .

The silence between them filled the air. Clare for her part was quite lost in her confused thoughts and Timothy had to repeat himself to get her attention when he finally spoke again.

'Why are you really here?' His voice was level and quiet but Clare felt she detected a timbre, a sort of controlled intensity, or was

48

she just getting touchy? She decided to ignore it.

'That's an odd question for you to ask as it was your letter that summoned me here,' she retorted tartly.

'Why do I have this feeling that there is something other than inspecting your inheritance keeping you here?'

Clare shrugged. 'I'm having a break — a week's holiday.'

'Working in a run-down florist's shop?'

Clare surprised herself by feeling annoyance at this remark. It was OK for her to criticize Flowers For The Journey but not for anyone else to do so. She smiled ruefully, realizing that she was reacting like a parent, or a devoted owner. She pushed down the thought, along with the random idea that there might be pluses to taking on this legacy after all. She pushed her empty coffee cup away and stood up.

'I had better get back to work. Thanks for lunch. I'll be in touch.' She walked swiftly away.

Mark was in the doorway looking down the street, but even as she saw him he turned and disappeared inside the shop. Clare felt irritated; was he watching her, timing the break she took for lunch?

'I haven't been quite half an hour,' she said

49

defensively, looking pointedly at her watch.

'Twenty-eight minutes, but I wasn't timing you. I just happened to notice.'

'Sure.' Clare didn't believe him. 'Timothy told me you are living in . . . ' She paused, realizing she had been about to say 'in my house'. She was still searching about for an alternative when he said it for her.

'Your house?' He looked at her and grinned and his rather morose expression vanished. Once more, Clare was struck by the extraordinary brilliance of his blue eyes.

She found herself smiling back. 'The house,' she corrected. 'How did you guess?'

'I didn't — I knew. Tim told me you were up here, so it didn't take much deduction to work out that you were Hester's niece checking up on things.'

'I see.' Somehow Clare felt his words put her in rather a bad light. Defiantly she tilted her chin and looked him in the eye. 'Mr Trimble says if I want to see the house I have to ask you.'

'I'm living there — caretaking. If you want to check the place out why don't you come back with me when we close the shop?'

Clare thought it hardly a gracious invitation and because he sounded as if he didn't care a damn whether she did or not, she replied, 'Yes — why don't I?'

Conversation between them was limited for the remainder of the afternoon. They were in fact almost busy. The stock of half-price cyclamens were going down and they sold several bunches of flowers. Looking round the shop space, which, after her vigorous tidying efforts, tended to look larger and therefore emptier, Clare decided that what was needed was more nonperishable stock. Vases, even ornaments, ceramic pots, perhaps. She let her mind wander over a range of items and was surprised when Mark interrupted her reverie by asking, 'Why the brown study?'

'Just wondering what we could put in here — you know, flower-connected items that wouldn't wilt or fade.'

Mark raised his eyebrows. 'Are you seriously thinking of taking over, then?'

'Oh, no, no, of course not . . . I don't see how . . . ' Her words trailed away. Timothy's suggestion that she could ask Mark to stay on as manager flitted through her mind but she shut down on the thought when she saw he was watching her. There was something about that bright blue gaze of his that she found disconcerting. She glanced at her watch — five o'clock, the time they closed according to the notice on the door. She remembered that he had said he could only employ her a few hours, yet she had been hard at it all day.

'Is there anything else?' She asked tentatively before she removed her overall.

Mark shook his head. 'No — I'll cash up and you can lock the door.' He turned his attention to the till. 'Hmm. The best day we've had for a long time,' Clare wasn't sure whether he was talking to her or himself. 'Let's go, then. You can follow me — you shouldn't lose me.'

Unlikely, Clare thought, as she watched him get into the mustard-coloured Beetle parked at the kerb. A short time later she drew up behind him outside a stone cottage on the edge of the little township. 'Oh!' she exclaimed involuntarily on the breath of a long drawn-out sigh. 'How lovely,' she whispered out loud. For a moment she just sat, hands on the steering wheel, a well of silence enveloping her as she turned off the engine, and gazed at the house, drinking in its tranquil charm.

The large, unevenly shaped and sized stones it was built of had mellowed with time so that they glowed in the early evening light. As the sun caught the front windows they sparkled and winked at her as if conveying a welcome message. Scented jasmine covered the front porch, its heady perfume sending its own greeting, and over the front fence wisteria, gnarled and twining, heavy with the

amethyst coloured blossom that was beginning to spill its colour on the sidewalk added
to its charm. Seeing Mark heading towards
her from his own parked vehicle, Clare
stepped out of the car and in a daze twisted
the key in the lock before turning back to face
the house again. It was not large — in fact, it
was definitely small — but built on to the side
was an extension in western red cedar. The
windows of this room were large, much larger
than those of the house itself.

Hazarding a guess, Clare asked, 'Is that a
studio? Was . . . did er . . . Miss McMaster
paint?' She stumbled over the words, assailed
by a shaft of unexpected guilt. She didn't
know a thing about the woman, and could
not think of her as her aunt, however far
removed, yet she had left her this perfect
dream house.

Mark nodded, giving her a strange look as
he did, as if, Clare thought, he had divined
her thoughts. He grunted something that
could have been 'Yes' and looked away from
her to grapple with the latch of the gate.
Clare followed him through, noting that the
house seemed to be set on a larger than
average block. The front garden was fairly
small but she could see that the back part,
separated from the front by the studio and a
tall picket fence running from it to the

boundary fence, went back quite a distance. As she stood there, a large hairy black and white creature bounded up, put his front paws on the top of the fence and, with lolling tongue and waving tail, grinned a welcome.

'Is that . . . the dog?'

'Meet Boris.' Mark's features split into a broad smile, seeing her expression.

'Do you want to see inside?' It was a grudging suggestion, rather than an invitation.

'I'd love to.' Clare's words faded out when she realized that Mark was opening a gate in the picket fence and obviously expected her to face the monster who stood between her and this dream house, literally as well as figuratively at this moment.

'He won't hurt you.' His voice was level, almost expressionless, but Clare did not miss the glint of malicious humour as he held the gate for her and stood back to let her go first. The dog seemed the size of a horse with his face almost level with her own.

'He's very . . . large.'

'He is,' Mark agreed. 'In fact, he is the same size as me. Boris . . . ' he called softly and, turning his hands back, tapped each of his own shoulders with the tips of his fingers. The dog immediately approached Mark and, rising on his hind legs, placed his front paws on the man's shoulders. 'You see, he is the same height as me.'

'Yes,' Clare agreed with some awe, 'I can see that.' She moved quickly away, heading for where she hoped there would be a door and with the fervent hope that Mark would not suggest to this monster that he check her out for size.

It was dim inside the house. Clare could imagine it cool on the hottest summer day. There was also a stillness about it, which she supposed was natural as no one had been in it all day. No, it was more than that, she admitted to herself. There was an atmosphere here, one of stillness and peace. She liked it.

'I suppose you want to see the whole house?' Mark's voice brought her back to the present with a jolt. She looked at him vaguely, the truculent note in his voice jarring.

'May I . . . please?' she answered eagerly, almost humbly.

It was not very large: just two bedrooms, a living room, a bathroom and a kitchen. All totally functional. It was also, she supposed, quite undistinguished, yet she felt a warm rush of feeling engulf her. It was as if she had come home after a long absence. With a mental shake Clare reminded herself that she was turning down this legacy. And the reason was outside in the form of that monstrous dog. She could no more move him into her Melbourne apartment than she could a horse, even if the terms of the will allowed her to.

'It's very nice.' She endeavoured to iron the enthusiasm out of her voice as she turned to the door. 'Thank you for showing me round.'

She drove back to her motel in Castlemaine, thinking about the house and the whole business of this extraordinary bequest that had come out of the blue. If only it could be split up. She was rapt in the house, pretty certain she didn't want a run-down flower shop and convinced she didn't want Boris.

3

The motel she had chosen had its own restaurant so she was able to have dinner without going out into the town. She was thankful for that for she found that she was both hungry and tired. Back in her room after a pleasant meal, she stretched out on the bed and fell asleep. Her mobile phone ringing woke her. 'Robert . . . ?' still muzzy with sleep, it took her a second or two to place his voice. The last few days had put her everyday life a million miles away. She knew she didn't want to see Robert again — ever — and she didn't want to talk to him now.

'I thought I might come up for a night. I could think up some reason, I'm sure.'

'No, it's not worth it. I — I'm coming back,' she lied, cursing her own inability to tell people unpleasant truths. 'And anyway I'm busy. I wouldn't be able to see much of you — it wouldn't be worth it,' she floundered on, digging herself into a deeper hole with every word she spoke.

'We would have the nights,' he pointed out, in a voice that would once have made her yearn for him.

'No,' She surprised herself with the sharpness of her tone, took a deep breath and went on, 'No, Robert. I don't want you to come, and I don't particularly want to see you when I get back.'

In the short silence that followed, Clare could imagine just how he looked, lips set into a thin line, doing his best to be patient and reasonable with her, making allowances. Before, when she'd been confronted with this expression, she had quickly gabbled an apology. Now she remained stubbornly silent.

'I see,' he said at last in a tone of voice that said that he didn't. 'We'll see how you feel about things when you get back. Goodnight, my dear.'

'I won't feel any different — ' Clare began, but he had hung up. Feeling frustrated and furious, she contemplated calling him back then thought better of it and switched off her phone instead. This, she knew, was Robert's way. If he couldn't win an argument he closed it. She thought back over their conversation: she had not told him the name of the motel, and with any luck he would not be able to contact her again if she kept her mobile turned off. She turned over to go back to sleep, but that was not so easy. Robert had stirred her thoughts, if not her body, and after tossing and turning, thumping the pillow and turning it over, she slid out of bed, pushed her arms into the light satin robe she had brought with her, filled the hot-water jug and clicked it on. While it boiled, she cruised through the available channels on the TV, but nothing interested her. She flicked it off and turned to the now boiling jug and made herself a coffee. Hungry, in spite of the good meal she had eaten earlier, she tore open one of the complimentary packets of biscuits and, taking them back to bed, propped herself up with pillows to sip, munch and think.

Clare ate the last biscuit, brushed the crumbs off the sheets and passed a hand over her eyes as if brushing away cobwebs before picking up her half-finished coffee. The gesture, which she had barely been aware of making, had indeed cleared her mind. Or was it the bright blue eyes of Mark Fisk that had prompted her determination to end her relationship with Robert?

She dismissed the thought as absurd and unworthy of herself. Her disillusion had begun before she ever came to this part of the world and set eyes on the man. She didn't even like him — he was arrogant and disagreeable — so why should the fact that he had extraordinary eyes influence her in any way? Thoughtfully sipping her coffee, she marvelled not that Robert's feet of clay were beginning to show but that she had not noticed them before.

She supposed she had believed his string of excuses and promises because she wanted to. She had even admired him when, in the early days of their relationship, he had explained that he could not possibly walk out on his marriage while his daughter, Annabel, was so young, not quite thirteen and settling into secondary school. 'Just wait a while,' he had begged, 'till she is a little older and can cope better.' Clare had waited — for two years. Annabel was now fifteen, and from what she knew of her, a remarkably self-contained and self-assured young lady. Robert had pointed out when she attempted to bring up the subject of their relationship and where — if anywhere — it was heading, that the teenage years were critical and she would soon be facing important exams. It would be too unsettling to walk out on her now.

Sitting up in bed drinking rapidly cooling coffee in a strange motel room, Clare reclaimed her life, though she didn't think of it like that. She would have said that she was tired of waiting around for a man who never intended to do anything about changing his way of life, She gulped down the remainder of the coffee, put the light out then slid down beneath the bedclothes. Her last waking thought was sympathy for Robert's wife for all the lies she had been fed, probably over many years. She did not delude herself that she had been the only illicit love in Robert's life.

★ ★ ★

When Clare arrived at the shop, Mark was already unloading fresh flowers from his yellow Beetle. Clare thought it looked a very inadequate vehicle for the job. Getting out of her own car, she greeted him and offered to help.

'Get this lot in water and arrange them,' he instructed her before turning to the cash register and getting it started for the day.

'Please would be a nice gesture,' Clare muttered to herself as she began filling buckets and containers. Mark watched her for a moment or two before silently adding price tags to the various arrangements. Clare stepped back, pleased with the effect. There were, she admitted, certain very satisfying moments in this job.

'You can put a couple of those buckets outside — carnations and irises.' Mark's curt order interrupted her pleasant reverie. Biting back a retort, reminding herself she was only the hired help, and temporary at that, Clare struggled out with two heavy buckets. Why couldn't he have told her to do this before? It would have been much easier when the buckets were empty. They made a bright splash of colour on the grey sidewalk; she hoped they would do their job of attracting customers.

They appeared to, for several customers came in for cut flowers. By midday Clare had decided she could easily tell who were locals and who were visitors to the area. Visitors didn't give her a second glance, locals looked at her with barely hidden curiosity: some even asked with a smile if she was new, and did she think she would like the job. Clare smiled and said she thought she would.

As before, Mark went for lunch first, leaving Clare in charge on her own again. She wished she had eaten more of the breakfast provided by the motel as her stomach began to rumble. She rather enjoyed being alone like this, moving things around, serving customers and fantasizing about actually owning the shop, and what she would do with it.

'Still here, I see.' She turned round from a flower arrangement Mark had done, which she privately thought needed improving. Timothy Trimble was standing just inside the door, smiling at her.

'Did you think I wouldn't be?' she retorted more sharply than she intended because he had made her jump.

Timothy shrugged. 'I wasn't sure.' After a pause, which she failed to fill, he added, 'I'll be at the same place as yesterday if you care to join me when you can.'

'Thanks,' Clare answered casually. It was kind of him, but she wasn't sure she really wanted to; this was only the second day he had asked her and already she was beginning to feel organized. But when Mark returned five minutes later, she found herself heading off towards the café and Timothy.

She selected a huge salad roll, its filling literally overflowing. 'That should stop a gap,' Timothy quipped as he handed it to her.

'It needs to — I'm starving.' She bit into it as she spoke, causing lettuce, cress and beetroot to drop out on to her plate. 'Working in there certainly beats sitting in an office for promoting a healthy appetite.'

'You like it?' He sounded surprised.

'I like it,' Clare affirmed, even more surprised to hear what she was saying and knowing she meant it. 'I went to see the house last night,' she added after a few minutes' solid chewing.

'And?' Timothy asked, his sandwich poised on its way to his mouth.

'And I like it — very much.' She was about to add 'It's my dream house . . . ' but something in his expression arrested her. Instead she turned her attention to the serious business of finishing off her salad roll without losing any of the contents.

'So . . . you will be taking up your inheritance?'

'Hold on . . . I didn't say that. There are a few other things to take into consideration.'

'Such as Boris?'

'Such as Boris,' Clare repeated after him. She was concentrating on licking butter off her fingers, and when she looked up she saw that Timothy was regarding her across the table with undisguised amusement. She flushed, guessing that he was amused by her unsophisticated table manners. 'Actually' — she pulled her cup of foamy cappuccino closer as she spoke and began absently spooning the chocolate froth off the top — 'I was going to get in touch with you. Surely there must be some way round this. I mean, it is just so ridiculous expecting me to give a home to that enormous dog when I live in a small, strictly-no-pet-allowed flat in Melbourne. I could scarcely smuggle a goldfish in there, let alone a monster like that.' She sipped her coffee in silence for a few minutes, savouring its flavour, which, she had to confess, was among the best she had tasted. 'Suppose Mark Fisk had him?' she suggested.

'Then he would also be entitled to the house and the shop. The terms of the will are clear.'

'What you mean in practical terms is that my cousin, several times removed, has actually left her entire estate to her dog.'

'That's about it.'

'I could contest it.'

'Fighting wills is always an expensive business,' he pointed out.

'Hmmm.' As a lawyer herself she knew that. She also knew who were the real winners in these cases — not usually the litigants. 'Ah well, as I don't particularly want this inheritance, there's no problem.' Clare flashed him a dazzling smile that belied her inner thoughts. After seeing what there was on offer she was not quite so convinced on that score. Nibbling at the borders of her mind was the insidious thought that maybe, just maybe, a total change of direction in her life might not be such a bad thing after all. She glanced at her watch. 'Better be off.' She pushed back her chair as she spoke. 'Thanks for the lunch.'

Hurrying back to the shop, she wondered why she didn't like Timothy more than she did. He was personable, charming and attentive, yet when she had realized he was collecting her once again for lunch she experienced a fleeting feeling of panic, a feeling she quickly repressed. And now as she walked as quickly as she could away from him, she had an irrational feeling of escape. She decided she was being neurotic. He was, as she had already told herself, a very nice man and moreover he was doing his very best to be helpful — wasn't he?

When Mark greeted her with 'Had lunch with our friendly family lawyer again?' she bridled quickly in his defence.

'Nothing wrong with that, is there? He is friendly. In fact, he has been very kind to me.' She squared her chin and looked directly into those eyes, not at all sure she liked their keen and penetrating gaze. She had an uncomfortable feeling that lying to Mark Fisk would be worse than useless. Suddenly and quite unexpectedly, he smiled. Clare caught her breath; it was as if he had touched her physically. She dragged her gaze away and began to fiddle with a flower arrangement.

'Yes, I am sure he has,' Mark said in a deadpan voice that gave nothing away.

How was it that this unfriendly, rude man could fluster her like he did? She went into the back room and collected broom, dustpan and brush to tidy up the detritus that seemed to have collected on the shop floor since they opened.

'Have you had anyone else after this job?' she asked casually as she swept.

'No — but then I've taken the notice down.'

'But — But I told you I was only here for the week, it could only be temporary, just until someone else comes along . . . ' She found her words petering out in the face of his silence.

Mark shrugged. 'I'll worry about that when you are no longer here,' he told her before turning to answer the phone. Clare could hear that he was taking down instructions for an order to be delivered. She took her brushes into the back and noticed a beautiful wreath that he had been making while she was out at lunch.

'Can you do the shop?' Mark asked her as he put down the phone. 'That was an order for a floral display to be sent to that new restaurant that is opening.'

'Sure,' Clare said. 'Go ahead — I can call on you if I get in strife out here.' She thought that highly unlikely; she was feeling more confident and competent dealing with the customers every minute. In fact, she was beginning to enjoy it.

She was deep in discussion with a

loquacious matron and feeling rather pleased as she had persuaded her to buy not only flowers but a crystal vase to go with them when Mark reappeared from the back, where he had been working on the orders.

'Harry will be coming any tick of the clock to pick up those flower arrangements. The addresses and the message to go on the cards are on the desk, can you write them and put them on? I have an appointment and I'm running late.'

Clare concluded the sale and hurried into the back to do his bidding. She carefully wrote the addresses on one side of each label, turned them over and wrote the messages on the other. *Best Wishes In Your New Venture* — obviously the flower arrangement for the restaurant — and *In Deepest Sympathy* on the other. She had them in her hand to tie on when she heard the shop door. That would be Harry to collect them, so she swiftly tied on the labels and carefully carried the arrangements out. As Harry took them to his van, another customer came in.

She was kept busy for the rest of the afternoon, and Mark only came back in time to cash up and close the shop. He looked agreeably surprised when he saw how much business she had done but beyond that made no comment. Clare, tired and disheartened, felt a little appreciation would have been nice. She said goodnight and hurried out to her car. Driving back to her motel in Castlemaine, she looked forward to a hot shower, and wished, fleetingly, that there were a tub in her bathroom. A long hot soak would have been great.

Driving into Castlemaine, it crossed her mind that it was odd that Timothy Trimble should bother to come all the way to Maldon just to share a brief sandwich lunch with her. She parked her car in the space outside her unit, noticing idly that another car was also there. As she stepped out and locked the door, a man stepped out of this car and beamed at her over the roof of it.

Oh no! The very last person she wanted to see!

'Hello, Clare.'

'Robert!' Her voice sounded sharp and strident, in direct contrast to his soft tone. 'What on earth are you doing here?'

'I've come to see you, my dear. I told you I hoped to make it for at least a night.'

Clare gave an involuntary shiver and pulled her jacket closer, but it wasn't so much the cooling evening air as the sense of being trapped. She told herself she was being absurd; this was Robert, who had been her lover for two years. She knew him as closely

69

and intimately as it was possible to know anyone outside marriage. Why then did she have to force herself forward into his orbit?

'Robert, I've had a busy day, I'm tired and . . . I'm hungry.' She walked towards the motel entrance with an apologetic shrug and an attempt at a smile.

'Do you want to eat here? Is it any good?' He slid a solicitous hand under her elbow and gently propelled her forward.

Clare nodded. 'Yes' was all she said as she allowed herself to be led into the motel foyer. Inside she turned to him. 'Will you get a table? It can get busy. I'll just freshen up.' She half expected him to follow her as she escaped to her own unit. It was absolutely true she did need to freshen up after the day working in the shop. She toyed with the idea of making her escape, simply getting into her car and driving away. But of course there was no point in it — all she would succeed in achieving was postponing the moment when she had to face Robert and tell him the truth. The truth. God, what was that? She no longer knew.

Ten minutes later, tidied, titivated and changed, she made her way back to the main building and the restaurant where she found Robert at a table for two in a quiet corner. He was studying the menu with morose concentration. He looked up when she reached the table. 'Are you sure you want to eat here? You wouldn't prefer to go somewhere else?'

'Quite sure. I'm tired and hungry and I don't feel like tramping all over the town looking for somewhere that you would consider better.'

'I would take the car. I wasn't expecting you to walk.'

Clare sighed softly in exasperation. Why on earth did Robert have to take every comment so damn literally? Either that or completely ignore anything and everything she said. She didn't bother to answer but concentrated on reading the menu.

'Well, if you insist on staying here, you'd better order. I'm having the roast lamb; they can't go far wrong with that.' He picked up the wine list and gave that his attention.

'I'll have steak and salad, and I don't want anything to drink, thank you.'

The waitress had just arrived at their table in response to an imperious click of the fingers from Robert and he went ahead and ordered a bottle of wine. Stifling her irritation, Clare marvelled that she had once admired his ability to always summon waiters and the masterful way he ordered for her as well as himself. Tonight it annoyed her.

'I'd just like water, please.' She spoke directly to the waitress.

'In that case bring me a lager instead of the bottle of wine,' Robert snarled, throwing her a look that Clare knew was intended to make her grovel with guilt. She ignored it. When he turned back to face her, she could see he was making a superhuman effort to charm. She put the menu down and leaned back in her chair to wait for the offending mineral water.

'Your holiday doesn't seem to be doing you much good.'

'I'm not exactly on holiday,' Clare retorted, thinking of her work in the shop.

When Robert raised his eyebrows and asked, 'How can you be not exactly on holiday? Surely either you are or you're not?

She knew she had made a mistake.

'I came here partly on business, then decided to stay on and give myself a bit of a break.'

'I see. And how much longer is this break of yours going to last?'

Clare didn't like being interrogated in this way but disguised her annoyance with a light shrug and a bantering tone. 'Oh, I don't know — till I feel ready to come back, I guess. What about you, Robert, why have you come up here?'

'To see you. Why else?'

'I find that strange. You broke our date on my birthday, but can find time to come all this way for the night.' Even as she spoke, Clare knew she sounded aggrieved and wished she hadn't said it.

'Come now, you know I couldn't help that, but I'm here now, and we can enjoy a pleasant little holiday together, surely?'

'Robert,' Clare said at last, fighting to keep down her rising annoyance, 'haven't you realized that I have been trying to tell you that I want a real break? In fact I want out. I — '

'Of course you don't. I know things have been hard on you sometimes, but — '

'Robert, haven't you heard a word I've said?' Clare asked in exasperation. It seemed the only way she could get through to him was to be brutally frank. 'I don't want to be the other woman any more, Robert.'

'You are not the other woman, you are *the* woman.'

'That sounds very nice, but you know it isn't true. For the last two years I've been in the background of your life. Well, I don't want it any more.' Clare stopped, appalled, knowing she wasn't coming over as she meant to. She sounded as if she was begging him for more — when what she wanted was less. His next words confirmed this.

'I know, Clare, and I'm sorry. I realize it has been tough for you. It has for me, too, But we've done the right thing; I wouldn't feel happy if we had messed up Annabel's life, and neither would you. Just a little while longer and then . . . ' He reached across the table for her hand, but feigning not to notice Clare withdrew it. How many times had she heard this record played over the last couple of years?

Clare sighed. 'Oh, Robert, you don't understand. I'm trying to tell you that our relationship is over.' She leaned back in her chair.

'I suppose you have got someone else, someone without ties. Do I know him?'

'There is no one else,' she snapped, hastily dismissing from her mind's eye a pair of startling blue eyes. 'Why is it so impossible for a man to accept that a woman might just want to be free and independent?'

'I always believed that was what you were.' He sounded, Clare thought, like a sulky adolescent.

'You thought wrong. I was neither, I was expected to be available when you wanted to see me, out of sight when you didn't Now, if you will excuse me . . . ' She pushed back her chair and rose to leave the restaurant. 'I'm sorry you have had this trip for nothing.'

Robert got to his feet so swiftly that his chair gave an angry scrape on the polished floor and looked for a moment as if it might topple right over. While he was straightening it, Clare hurried to the door, planning to get to her unit. She made it from the restaurant but at the outer door she collided head on with a man coming in.

'Oh, I'm so sorry — Oh, it's you!' she stammered as she looked up into Timothy's startled face, almost pushing him back out through the door in her urge to escape.

Looking over her shoulder, Timothy saw Robert. 'Are you having trouble, Clare?' he asked.

'No — I mean yes, yes, I am.' She had been offered a straw, she might as well grab it and make the most of it. She caught Timothy's sleeve. 'Can you — would you — come to my room?' she gasped.

He looked startled, but stayed by her side as she hurried to her unit and quickly pushed the key into the lock. Inside she slammed the door shut and leaned back on it with a sigh. 'I — I'm sorry about that,' she stammered. 'Thank you for co-operating.'

'Not at all. I regularly help damsels in distress.'

Clare managed a smile. 'Well, thank you — I'm glad you were there. I . . . I won't keep you . . . You were going in to dinner?'

'I was, and if you're sure you'll be all right now, I'd better go. I'm meeting someone.' He moved over to the window and looked out. 'He's getting in his car.'

Clare heard a car door slam with some force, followed by an engine being revved and the sound of a moving car receding. She sighed with relief.

'He's gone,' Timothy said, rather unnecessarily. He moved to the door, turning towards her. 'Rather an unpleasant fellow, I thought. Do you know him?'

'Yes — I mean no. Well, just slightly,' Clare found herself burbling. Timothy raised his eyebrows in mild enquiry.

'I — he — I don't think he meant any harm . . . '

Why on earth was she defending him, and why had she lied? Two years of knowing anyone as closely and intimately as she had known Robert was scarcely 'slightly'. Illogically she now felt annoyed with Timothy for his unflattering remark. She moved over to the door to close it behind him. 'Thanks, anyway,' she managed to say before she firmly closed and locked the door.

4

Damn! What on earth did he have to follow her here for? Clare demanded of herself, regretful that she had left the dining-room so precipitously — she was hungry. She checked out what the motel had to offer in the room; coffee or tea and a small packet of biscuits. In the absence of anything else, that would have to do.

She flicked the electric jug on, kicked off her shoes and threw herself down in the easy chair, unwrapping the biscuits while she waited for the water to boil. She had a sneaking feeling that she had behaved with less than poise and sophistication. Her annoyance with herself turned to anger at Robert: how dare he follow her up here and act in such a proprietary manner? Their two-year relationship didn't give him owner-ship of her, even if he thought it did.

Thinking about this caused her tiredness to give way to restlessness, so she picked up the remote control of the TV set and surfed through the channels, hoping to find something of interest. But nothing held her attention, which kept returning to her problems: what to do about Robert, and whether to accept her inheritance.

As far as Robert was concerned, she had decided even before she came here, she had had enough of being the second woman in his life. From now on it would be number one or nothing.

The inheritance was not so easy. If only this unknown great aunt of hers had not been so inflexible. She would dearly love to be the owner of that dream cottage. Maldon was near enough to Melbourne to allow her to spend most weekends up here. But it seemed that monster hound was in residence, and possession was nine points of the law. The flower shop she was ambiguous about. She had never thought of giving up her legal career to run a business, but there was no denying that she was quite enjoying herself, and it certainly represented a challenge. Being a divorce lawyer could be a bit of a depressing job at times. She reflected that no one entered marriage with the idea of it failing; on the contrary they all seemed to imagine it was the open sesame to a life of happy ever after. She supposed that what went wrong was something like her own disenchantment with her relationship with Robert. For the first time she was thankful that they were not married.

There was nothing on the television to distract her from her own thoughts so she took the only other option and went to bed, only to dream an absurd fantasy about living in the cottage with Boris, only somehow their roles were reversed and although he was still very definitely a dog he was equally definitely in charge, and she was the one who was behaving like, and treated as, an animal.

She woke up feeling quite put out but determined to see Timothy and insist that somehow the terms of the will were bypassed.

She went straight to the offices of Knight, Boyd and Trimble and waited what seemed an incredibly long ten minutes, only to be told that Timothy Trimble was not yet in and anyway his appointment book was full for the day. Clare left a message that she needed to talk to him and hoped that he would turn up at lunchtime.

'You are very late this morning,' Mark snapped when she arrived at the shop.

Clare opened her mouth to defend herself then shut it again when she remembered her ambiguous position. She was not a bona fide employee, nor was she a bona fide employer. She mumbled a brief apology without an explanation, then went into the back room for an overall, collected a broom and started sweeping up. Mark scowled at her before going into the office to answer the phone. A few minutes later he reappeared. 'Come here!'

Clare turned, startled both by the volume of his voice and the fury in it. She propped the broom against the wall and before she reached the office he had turned away to answer the phone again. This time she heard him speaking in a conciliatory voice, even apologizing profusely to someone. This seemed so unlike what she thought she had learned about him that she unashamedly listened and was unprepared when he replaced the receiver with exaggerated care and turned on her with an explosion of fury.

'My God, Clare, I thought you were supposed to be an intelligent woman!'

She opened her mouth, intending to say that she wasn't supposed to be, she was, but before she could say a word in her defence against what seemed a totally unwarranted attack, Mark stormed, 'How could you — how could you do anything so impossibly unbelievably dumb? So crassly stupid?' He glared at her and Clare quivered before the fury blazing from those incredible eyes of his. Some slightly detached part of her mind noted that the blue seemed to have faded, so that they looked pale and glacial. As she gaped at him, his lips tightened into a thin line and with cutting sarcasm he went on, 'Or maybe you are not quite so stupid. Maybe there is some hidden agenda in your idiocy that I can't see but will ultimately work to your advantage.'

Clare drew herself up, squared her shoulders, jutted her chin and with a greater effort than she would have liked him to know, looked him in the eye.

'I have not the faintest idea what you are talking about. Please explain.'

'Oh, I'll explain all right.' He leaned forward for greater emphasis and the illogical thought flitted through Clare's mind that he had a good courtroom manner, before she remembered that for once she was not facing another lawyer in an antagonistic situation. 'Do you happen to remember that I asked you to put the cards on a couple of items I had made up ready for delivery?' He paused and fixed his unwavering stare on her face.

'Of course I remember, and I did it — '

'Oh, you did it — a simple little job that anyone, anyone with a modicum of intelligence, should be capable of doing.'

'Yes . . . ' Clare agreed, wondering what all this was leading up to. She knew she had put the cards on — she had written them most carefully and tied them on just as Harry arrived to collect them for delivery.

81

'Do you remember what they were?'

'Of course I do — a wreath and a floral arrangement for a new restaurant opening up. I thought they were both quite beautiful. I was most impressed.'

'You were? Well, the recipients were not at all impressed. In fact, they were quite annoyed.'

'But why? I wrote the messages you had jotted down most carefully — '

'And were you equally careful when you put them on? Did you for, instance, check the addresses or bother to make sure you had the right message with the right address?'

'Oh, my God!' Clare clapped a hand over her mouth as the inference of what Mark was saying sank in. 'I didn't . . . couldn't . . . could I?'

'You could, and you did.'

Clare thought back and remembered the gist of the two messages. 'Then the new restaurant got 'Deepest sympathy' and . . . and the dear departed was wished 'good luck in their new venture'.' She looked down at her feet and fought the rising tide of hysterical amusement threatening to overwhelm her. 'I'm very sorry,' she mumbled, before turning away to resume her sweeping.

'Clare!' She was forced to turn back. 'I suppose, if you subscribe to a belief in the hereafter, it might not be so … er … inappropriate, what do you think?' He sounded serious enough but when she turned to face him, Clare saw that his eyes had lost their glacial look and even twinkled slightly.

She nodded, then, unable to control herself any longer, let out a great guffaw of amusement. 'Have I got the sack?' she asked.

'No,' he told her when his own mirth had died away, 'but I have probably lost my job.'

'What do you mean?'

'Well, unless a few more people share our warped sense of humour that was probably the final nail in the coffin of a dead business. Anyway,' he added as if the thought had only just occurred to him. 'I can't sack you — it's your shop. I guess I owe you an apology.'

'It's not my shop, and it never will be, much as I would love to see the business turn around and be a success.' She was surprised to hear herself say that; even more to know that she really meant it.

★   ★   ★

'It's the most absurd thing I have ever come across,' Clare protested. 'I don't understand how you could even allow such a will to be drawn up, but since you have you know as well as I do that there are ways we could get

83

round it. We're both lawyers. If we put our heads together . . . ' Clare's voice trailed away as she looked across the desk and saw Timothy sit a little straighter in his chair. His expression tightened.

'I understand, Clare, that you specialize in divorce?' Clare nodded slightly. 'I must assure you that this firm is a respectable law firm with a very solid reputation.' He paused here to lend weight to his already ponderous words, and Clare could not resist interjecting with a sweet smile.

'You don't do divorces, then?'

'Well, yes, we do. But I personally don't handle that side of our work. We have a junior partner for that.' He managed to look both aggrieved and affronted. 'As I was saying, we have a very solid reputation and there is no way we could be persuaded to deviate in any way from our client's wishes.' Clare thought he sounded unbearably pompous and was seized with a wild desire to tell him so and enliven the telling with some choice expletives.

'All the same, I am surprised that you allowed anyone to make such a will,' she contented herself with remarking.

'If I didn't know it already, I would deduce from that remark that you did not know your aunt at all.' Pompous idiot, Clare thought, but merely smiled across the desk. 'She was a woman who knew her own mind,' he continued, adding with heartfelt emphasis, 'A very strong-minded woman indeed, and far from easy to deal with. She had been a client with Knight, Boyd and Trimble for a very long time. She was Mr Knight's client until he . . . er . . . passed away, and then she became Mr Boyd's till his retirement, when I took on the responsibility of handling her legal affairs.'

'You inherited her, then?' A thought crossed Clare's mind. 'What about Knight and Boyd, have they been replaced or — '

'No, they have not.' Timothy Trimble spoke curtly and began gathering up papers on his desk, hoping, Clare thought, to terminate this conversation.

'Then Knight, Boyd and Trimble is actually just Trimble, and the junior partner who handles divorces?'

He went on shuffling and organizing, or disorganizing, the papers on his desk and as the silence lengthened Clare thought either he had not heard or he simply didn't intend to answer her question.

'He handles that side completely — I must say I find it rather distasteful.' Clare thought he looked at her as he said it as if he was finding her equally distasteful.

85

'But don't you find that side of legal work is growing, quite rapidly in fact?'

Timothy Trimble knocked his gathered papers together on the desk and looked across at her. 'Are you telling me how to run my practice, Miss . . . er . . . Davenport? Or are you perhaps applying for a post here?' His smile was thin and his eyes cold. 'I understand your job at the florist shop is only temporary?'

'Heavens, no, of course I'm not applying for a position in your firm! And I had no intention of suggesting you were anything but efficient. As for my so-called job in the shop . . . ' Her words trailed off in a shrug as she realized, too late after her protestations, that this little exchange was Timothy Trimble's attempt at humour. Or was it? She had noticed that she became Miss . . . er . . . Davenport when she annoyed him.

She got up to leave, feeling that she had not just been side-tracked but actually beaten in an argument. She was not used to feeling that and she did not like it. 'I came here to discuss the possibility of coming to some reasonable sort of compromise about this d — this will.' She managed to bite off the swear word, mild as it was, fearing it would do her less than no good. 'But it seems you are not even prepared to discuss it with me.'

'Please, Miss . . . er . . . Clare, don't be hasty. I merely reiterated my client's — my *late* client's — wishes. Won't you sit down again?' He gestured to the chair and reluctantly Clare turned back and sat down. 'Perhaps you could explain to me exactly what the problem is?'

'The problem is . . . ' Clare spoke slowly and carefully as if explaining to a deaf person. 'The problem, Mr Trimble, is that I have inherited a legacy that seems to me to have impossible terms, or at any rate terms that I, personally, do not feel I can accede to. Therefore it seems I cannot inherit anything. Yet presumably your client wanted me to inherit, or why else mention me at all in her will?'

Timothy Trimble leaned back in his chair, revolved it a quarter turn each way, leaned back again, considering her, then leaned forward and folded his hands in front of him on the desk. By this time Clare was beginning to lose her cool to the point where she was feeling quite uncomfortable. This was an unusual sensation for her; she was more accustomed in her interviews with clients to be the one putting others on the spot. With a shock she realized that he was using the same tactics she used herself. The thought made her smile. Seeing the slight curve of her lips,

Timothy looked irritated and leaned forward a little more. But when he spoke Clare had the impression he was having some difficulty choosing the right words.

'You are right — she did. At least I think she did — yes, of course she did. In fact, I would say she was quite anxious that her only blood relation should be the one to inherit her home and her business. On the other hand, she was also extremely fond of young Mark Fisk.'

Clare raised an eyebrow. 'Not so young, surely?' Clare guessed him to be at least her own age if not a little older. 'Now you have mentioned him, perhaps you could explain to me just how he fits into the picture?'

'Mark? Oh, he is the son of an old friend of your aunt and he has been very helpful to her over the years. Even now, after her death, he is caretaking her house and shop and — '

'Looking after her dog,' Clare cut in, irritated by this rambling non-explanation which seemed to be leading nowhere.

'Exactly. And as you yourself have pointed out, that is the heart of the matter. Your aunt was extremely attached to the dog and very concerned about his well-being after she passed away. He is a rather large dog and she feared it would be difficult for him to be

rehoused through any of the normal channels.'

'Normal channels?'

'The RSPCA, that sort of thing.'

'I can imagine,' Clare said drily, surprised
at the sudden pang she felt at the thought of
that large and indubitably magnificent dog
homeless and unwanted. After all, she didn't
want him. 'Mark seems very attached to him.
Couldn't he just give him a home?' she asked
hopefully.

'If he had a home I have no doubt he
would. But as you must have realized, Mark is
living in what, according to the will, is actually
the dog's home,' He smiled beatifically at her
across the expanse of his desk and Clare had
the uncomfortable feeling that the conversation had swung right round to square one and
she had got absolutely nowhere.

'What you are telling me' — she got to her
feet as she spoke — 'is that there is no way
you are going to make it possible for me to
have any part of this legacy?'

Timothy shrugged helplessly. 'Clare, you
are a lawyer — you must see my position. I
have to respect my client's wishes.'

'Has it crossed your mind that I could
contest this?'

'Of course it has, and of course you could,
but you and I know that the only people who

really win in such cases are the lawyers.'

Clare did know. By the time extensive legal proceedings had whittled away the funds, there was often little to fight about. She held out her hand to him across the desk. 'I guess there is little point in my taking up any more of your time. Thank you for your help.' She meant to sound sarcastic but only succeeded in sounding pathetic and defeated.

'Goodbye.' He stood up now. 'Enjoy the remainder of your . . . er . . . holiday here.'

Clare thought about her work in the flower shop — hardly a holiday yet she knew she was going to miss it. Maybe it would be better to go back now and not stay the week out. With a slight shrug and a mumbled 'thanks', she turned and left the office of Timothy Trimble, wishing in that moment that she had never set foot in it.

Her first impulse was to get in her car, drive back down the hghway to Melbourne and resume her normal life and forget all about this little interlude. But conscience or something made her turn the car towards Maldon instead. It would, she felt, be churlish to leave without at least giving Mark some sort of an explanation. After all, she had agreed to help him out in the shop for a week.

She found him poring over the books,

looking anything but happy. When he looked up and saw her, his expression lightened momentarily and Clare found herself smiling back. He scowled down at the paperwork in front of him and growled, 'Still here, then. When you didn't come in at the usual time I thought you had gone back. I wouldn't blame you — after all, it can't be much fun working in a shop as run down as this one with no hope of taking it over and making a go of it. I don't know how much longer I can stick it out myself.'

'How did you know I have no hope of taking it over?' Clare's legal mind snapped on to what she felt was the crucial point in this gloomy monologue.

'Everyone knows about your aunt's will. A right mess she's made of things, if you ask me.'

'I'm not asking you,' Clare snapped, suddenly defensive of this unknown relative who only a short while back she herself had been mentally cursing. 'Anyway, why are you bothered? You're all right; a comfortable home to live in with nothing more onerous to do than look after a dog.'

'And this bloody shop,' Mark snapped back. 'If I could either ditch it or make it pay it wouldn't be so bad.'

'Why can't you?'

'Why can't I what?'

'Either — both — anything.'

'I can't ditch it because it has to stay with the rest of the legacy for the time being. I can't make it pay because there is no money available to put into it and I am neither a florist nor, it would seem, a businessman — and I guess you need to be both.'

'Just what are you then?' Clare demanded belligerently.

She was surprised to see his expression of frustration and rage become what she could only describe as 'sheepish'. He looked round the shop with a hopeless air, then down at the sets of figures he had been grappling with before slamming the folders and books shut and mumbling, 'An accountant, a bloody accountant, that's what I'm *supposed to be*, and I can't see any way to balance these books.'

Clare couldn't have been more surprised if he had announced that he was a strongman in a circus. 'My God, you really are hopeless!' she burst out, suddenly so irritated she wanted to yell and storm, hit him over the head with the wretched books he had been gloomily gazing at — anything to wake him out of his negativity.

'You are missing the point,' he told her wearily. 'It's just because I am an accountant that I can see what a real mess this bloody business is in.'

Clare stared at him, realizing that what he said was quite true. All the same . . . 'Come on, let's do something about this place, spruce it up, make it look a bit more interesting,' she urged. 'I've still got a few days left before I have to go back to Melbourne.' Whatever was she talking about? Timothy had almost convinced her there was no future for her here, so why bother? There was no sensible reason; probably just cussedness on her part and a dislike of giving up on anything before she had given it her very best shot at least. She didn't like seeing Mark look so defeated either. 'Between us we can at least make it look as if it hasn't entirely given up the ghost!' It was idiotic and quixotic, her logical mind told her, yet she knew it was what she wanted to do more than anything in the world at this point in time.

Feeling embarrassed and rather foolish, especially as Mark merely returned to his accounts, Clare flounced into the back room, snatched down an overall and collected sweeping tools.

As she swept and tidied she wondered why on earth she was bothering to do this, and why she cared about the shop or Mark, who was still frowning and sighing over his wretched accounts. Without warning her irritation bubbled back to the surface.

'For God's sake, why don't you use a computer?'

'A computer?'

'That's what I said. You have heard of them, I suppose? They were invented last century and — '

'I don't use a computer because . . . ' Mark spoke slowly and clearly as if he was talking to someone either stone deaf or very ignorant. 'I can't afford one, or rather the shop can't afford one. If you look at these books you will see that.'

Clare dropped the broom and marched across to the table where the books were spread out. 'I'm looking. All I can see is a set of squiggles partly in black and partly in red. Biro, I see. I'm surprised you aren't using a quill pen.'

'Very funny!' Mark slammed the offending books and papers together, pushed them all into a somewhat tatty folder and stood up. 'And yes, before you ask, I can use a computer. It just so happens I have left mine in W.A., but as it isn't a laptop it would have been a bit cumbersome to transport.' He glared at Clare and she noted absently that his eyes were looking glacial again. Their gaze locked for a moment and to her fury she

94

found her breath catching in her throat. She was about to offer the loan of her laptop, which she seldom, if ever, used, when Mark's eyes shifted to the door. She turned and saw a van had drawn up outside and the driver was bringing in a load of cyclamen plants. Didn't Mark's imagination get any further than that, she wondered, but bit her tongue before she expressed her thoughts aloud. He seemed to have heard them, however.

'They sell.' He spoke tersely through gritted teeth before turning to the man and signing the docket. To Clare's relief he had also brought in some bunches of fresh flowers. Without comment she took them and arranged them in buckets of water and grouped the cyclamens around them. The effect, if a tad sparse, was at least colourful.

They resumed their chores in silence. Clare finished her sweeping and arranging what stock there was, and after a few minutes Mark put his papers away and wrote out the prices for the new stock. The somewhat oppressive silence was only broken by the occasional customer wandering in.

After an hour of this silence, Clare emerged from the back room, purse and car keys in her hand. 'What are you doing?' Mark demanded.

'Going.' She could be as terse as him if need be. 'There is obviously little point in my staying.'

Mark stared at her for a moment, then mumbled, 'Look, I'm sorry, I didn't mean to be disagreeable — you have every right to express your opinion. It's just that — well, I can't help but feel this is such a hopeless and rather pointless effort keeping this business on, trying to make it viable.'

Clare stared back. 'I'm sorry too,' she admitted at last. 'I shouldn't have gone off like that — I can see it isn't really your fault. It's just that, well, I suppose I was feeling frustrated after my interview with Timothy.' She held out her hand to him. 'Pax?'

He hesitated for so long that she almost withdrew it, then with a sudden grin that illuminated his features he gripped it so hard she almost yelped. 'Pax!' he agreed.

'I think — ' he said after a moment.

'Why don't we — ' Clare began at exactly the same moment. They both stopped. 'You first,' she told him.

'I think we should put our heads together and see if we can work out something to make the place pay. And you?'

'I was going to say much the same thing. Why don't we use our combined intelligence to see if anything can be done instead of slinging off at each other like a couple of kids?'

It was a good suggestion in theory, but in practice it resulted in them working in silence. 'I think we should computerize,' Clare said at last.

'Computerize what, and what with?'

'Well, the business, of course.'

'We need to work out how to make it a viable business that can afford a computer first,' Mark pointed out, his tone of voice suggesting that he was trying hard to be patient with a very stupid person. It was not lost on Clare.

'Hasn't it occurred to you that if we were a bit more efficient in our running of it then it might — just might — become a viable business?'

They were interrupted here by a customer coming in for not one but two cyclamens. Clare was forced to admit that even if they were not very adventurous or imaginative, they did sell. Moreover, unlike cut flowers they did not have such a limited shelf life.

They spent the remainder of the morning bickering ineffectually and tossing ideas back and forth. The trouble was that each and every idea they put forward required capital to put it into action.

Clare wondered if Timothy would be at the

café at lunchtime; she sincerely hoped not. She was relieved when Mark suggested that he go out and collect salad rolls so that they could continue their discussion while they ate.

'What, exactly, did you hope to gain by going to see Timothy Trimble?' Mark asked between bites. 'You won't move him, you know.'

'So it seems.' Clare nodded gloomily. 'I just hoped there was some way round the impasse of the dog so that I could inherit.'

'What would you do then? Sell?' Mark's voice was sharp.

'Yes — no — I don't know.' She paused. 'I might put you in as manager.'

'And I might refuse the position.'

Clare looked at his shuttered face and was filled with sudden irritation and frustration. What the hell was she doing here, sitting in this pathetic shop eating a salad roll between bouts of sweeping up, tidying stock and serving the odd customer? She was supposed to be on holiday; she must have taken leave of her senses. Damn Aunt Hester for ever existing, never mind landing her with this problem. Well, she didn't want it. She was through with it — she was leaving.

'I've had enough,' she said, getting to her feet and glaring at Mark as he munched on the last mouthful of his roll with an expression of deep gloom.

'Good — because there isn't any more,' he told her.

'I'm not talking about food, as you very well know. I'm talking about this bloody shop, the house, the dog, everything, even you. I'm going.'

'Hey, hang on, you said you would stay the week. There's still a day and a half to go,' Mark protested.

'Too damn bad!' Clare shot back. Turning her back on him, she went into the back room to collect her things.

'What about your wages?' Mark asked when she reappeared.

'Keep them — put them in the kitty towards a computer.' She flounced out, discomfited by the realization that that was exactly what she was doing and that she had lost her cool. Her exit was not improved by nearly colliding with an incoming customer.

She slammed into her car and drove back to her motel to pack her belongings and settle her account. Then she had second thoughts; she didn't have to be back in the office till Monday morning so why not enjoy a bit of a holiday first? She felt she deserved it, and she was in no hurry to return to her everyday life.

5

In her motel room, Clare flung herself down on the bed. She felt as despondent as Mark had looked earlier. She tried telling herself there was no need to feel bad about the situation. After all, only a short while back she had known nothing about this inheritance, and she had been perfectly satisfied with her life as it was, hadn't she? She would simply be where she was before she got that wretched letter from the irritating Mr Timothy Trimble. No, not quite — for it seemed she had managed to quarrel with Robert. She supposed a suitable apology would bring him back into her life — if she wanted him. On the thought that she didn't, and if nothing else she had enjoyed the relative freedom of this week, she dropped off into a doze, tired after the physical work of the morning.

The bedside phone ringing woke her with a start. 'There is a gentleman here to see you,' the girl in reception informed her. 'Shall I direct him to your room?'

'No, don't do that, I'll be right there,' Clare told her, wondering as she pushed her feet into her shoes and ran a comb through her hair which of them it was. Surely not Robert? Then it had to be Timothy Trimble.

'You!' she spluttered when she saw that it was neither but Mark who was waiting for her in the reception area.

'You are still here, then?'

'Obviously,' Clare snapped in her effort to appear cool, calm and collected instead of totally ruffled by his unexpected appearance.

'Will you have dinner with me tonight? Sort of peace offering?'

'Where?' Clare asked, thinking even as she spoke that if anyone should be making this gesture it should be her. In an effort to make amends she said, 'Will you come here and have dinner with me?'

'No.' He shook his head emphatically. 'I would like you to come and have it with me — at the cottage. I think we need to continue the dialogue we started earlier.'

Clare studied him: she didn't think much good could come of any more discussion, but she nodded. 'All right . . . what time?'

'Give me an hour.'

Clare looked at her watch. 'I'll see you around seven,' she told him.

It was a minute before seven when she drew up outside the cottage. Unwilling to appear eager, she switched off the engine and stayed in the car with her hands resting on the steering wheel, her eyes on the cottage. As she gazed at it she was overwhelmed by a feeling of familiarity. She knew this house, she had seen it somewhere before; or dreamed of it. She sighed, picked up her bag and opened the door. Of course it was familiar, she *had* seen it before — only a few nights ago. But she was frowning slightly as she locked her car. She couldn't rid herself of the feeling of déjà vu.

When she saw that Mark had come out and was watching her, Clare felt foolish. How long had he been there?

But all he volunteered was a cheery 'Hi!' as she walked to meet him. She returned his greeting and they walked in a silence that was companionable rather than uncomfortable. Boris was leaning on the top of the fence dividing the front garden from the back yard. Standing there on his hind legs, paws on the top of the fence, he looked not only very large but also rather human, and Clare forgot her resentment of the dog as her lips curled in a smile of amusement. His tail began to wag furiously.

'See, he remembers you.'

'The feeling is mutual,' Clare said drily. 'I am hardly likely to forget him under the circumstances, am I?'

Mark led the way to a decorative wrought-iron garden setting — two chairs and a table — on the front veranda. 'Take a seat and we'll have a drink. I won't make you beard the monster this time.' He grinned at her. 'How does the idea of a nice cool Riesling grab you? Or would you prefer beer or a soft drink?'

'Wine, please,' Clare replied, agreeably surprised that he should offer such a civilized option. She relaxed into her chair while Mark fetched the drinks; it was not a hard thing to do in this tranquil setting. It already felt familiar to her, and she wished she could believe that it was a premonition foretelling a time when it would be totally familiar in all its aspects. She was frowning slightly, wondering at her feeling for this house, when Mark placed a glass in front of her and a small bowl of nuts. Clare looked up to smile her thanks and was surprised to meet his intent stare, but only briefly for he quickly turned away and, sitting down opposite, he picked up his own glass. She mumbled her thanks and lowered her eyes as she, too, sipped at the cool liquid.

'Mmmm, good,' she said appreciatively.

He nodded in acknowledgement of her approval. 'It's a local wine. You were frowning when I came out with the drinks — why?'

Taken by surprise at the direct question, Clare found herself answering without pausing to dissemble. 'I was wondering why this place seemed vaguely familiar to me — then I thought maybe it was premonition rather than memory.'

Mark snorted with wry amusement 'Ever hopeful, Clare?' Both his tone and his smile were faintly derisive and she bridled slightly.

'No, just puzzled.'

'You must have a very long memory, that's all.'

'Long memory? What do you mean? I never saw this house till a few days ago.'

'Actually you did, but I shouldn't have thought it would have made any impression on you. You were very young at the time, I believe.'

'What on earth are you talking about? I've told you — I've never been here before. Not in this life anyway,' she finished facetiously.

'You were brought here as a small baby — very small. A few months old at the most.'

'That is absurd. If I was only a few months old I wouldn't remember anyway. Who told you that?'

'No one. I remember.'

'Yeah, sure,' she drawled, intending to sound sarcastic. 'You're just making it up. I was never here so how could you remember?'

She watched him raise his glass to his lips then, leaning back in his chair, lift his glass in a sardonic toast before smiling at her over the rim.

'Explain,' she snapped, adding almost inaudibly, 'if you can.'

'You were brought here by your parents. I was here at the time with my mother — I was about three years old. You couldn't walk. I was disappointed about that — I thought you were coming to play with me.'

Clare did a quick mental calculation and decided he must be about two years older than her. Not that that mattered; what was important was the fact that she was not fantasizing, that she had been here before. 'My parents brought me here? Whatever for?'

'To show you to your great aunt, I suppose.'

'What were you doing here?'

'I lived here.'

'Lived here!' Clare was startled. 'You mean in this house? You lived here as a small boy?'

'Yup.'

Clare was seized with a wild desire to get up and shake the information out of him. There he sat making these remarks that raised more questions than they answered, giving monosyllabic answers. 'Explain!' she demanded.

'All in good time. Dinner should be ready — I hope you like mushroom risotto?'

Clare nodded. 'I love it,' she told him.

'Good, because that's what you're getting. Come in and eat and you can ask your questions then.'

Inside he motioned her to a place at the kitchen table which was tastefully set for two, refilled her glass and then busied himself collecting the meal from the stove and serving it out. Clare could hardly contain her impatience. 'Tell me why you were living here,' she demanded when he finally sat down opposite her.

'My mother was Hester McMaster's housekeeper.'

'And your father?' The question was out before she stopped to think that maybe she was being too probing.

'I had no father,' he told her curtly.

'What about my father? You said my parents brought me.'

He nodded. 'I remember feeling so envious of you, having a father, and he seemed nice, kind and gentle. He had a beard, I remember.'

Clare sighed. 'Yes, he was, but you had no cause to envy me — I don't remember anything of my father for the first six years of my life. In fact, I don't ever remember having

106

two real parents — that is, at the same time.' That was true. Until she was seven years old it had just been her and her mother, and of course the uncles, a succession of them. Just as she got used to one (she never got fond of any of them), they would go and after a while another one took their place. Then, quite suddenly, it was her mother who wasn't there any more. Killed in an accident, someone said. A neighbour looked after her till, to her relief, her father reappeared to claim her. But her joy at having a father was soon diminished when she discovered she had to share him with a new wife. But not for too long, after a period of loud and stormy rows when Clare pulled the bedclothes over her head in order to shut out her stepmother's strident voice complaining about having a sulky brat of a step-daughter thrust on her. It was some time before Clare realized that was her, and by then the stepmother had gone, just like the uncles did, and from then on for the most part it was just her and her father.

As she grew up, Clare became convinced that it was something about her that drove everyone away and she strived ceaselessly to justify her existence by being the sort of daughter her father wanted her to be. As what he seemed to want most of all was to see her achieve academic excellence, go to college and 'make something of herself', she made a lawyer of herself. Unfortunately he never knew, for he died during her last year at college.

She came out of her brown study to agree with Mark. 'Yes, you're right about my father, he was kind and gentle. In fact, that was the root of a lot of the trouble.'

'How so?'

'He never stood up for anything, or anyone, not himself or me, especially not me.' For a few moments she was lost in her own memories, then she said thoughtfully, 'It must have been about that time that my mother left him and took me with her. I didn't see him again until my mother was killed and he collected me to live with him. I was seven years old at the time, and by then my father had a new wife.'

'That can't have been easy for anyone.'

Clare looked up sharply. 'No, I suppose not.' Until then she had always felt that the person it was hard on was herself; she had not considered the effect it must have had on the others involved.

'How did you all adjust?'

Clare shrugged. 'Oh, we coped . . . ' Her face closed up as she added, 'When my father didn't want to send me away to boarding school, she left. I felt very bad about that. I wouldn't have minded boarding school so much — as it was I felt I was to blame for her going.' She told him all this in a flat, expressionless voice and when she faced him across the table, her expression told him that the subject was now closed. 'Tell me, if you can, something about my Aunt Hester. What was she really like, and do you have any idea why I never saw her again? Even more, why do I find myself her reluctant heir? Why didn't she leave it to someone else? You, for instance?'

It was a provocative remark, but if Mark was provoked he took good care not to show it.

'She probably felt, and I agree with her, that by giving me a home and seeing me through my education she had done all she needed for me. She was a remarkable woman in many ways but not always very easy.' His tone of voice implied that was all he intended to say. His next words confirmed this. 'We had better get our thinking caps on and see if there is any way we can make the shop a viable proposition. After all, that is what you are here for.'

'Yes,' Clare agreed, then with a sudden spurt of irritation, 'I've given you my life history but you haven't told me anything about yourself, or even about my aunt.'

'I hope you like strawberries?' Mark asked, as if she hadn't spoken.

'Yes, I love them, thanks.' She felt obliged to reply with at least a modicum of good manners; she was, after all, his guest.

'Cream, ice-cream, frozen yoghurt — or a bit of everything?'

'Oh, a bit of everything, please.'

'Good idea — I will too.' He placed a small glass bowl almost overflowing with strawberries, ice-cream and frozen yoghurt in front of her, then placed a small jug of cream at her side. Only when he was seated opposite her and had helped himself to the cream did he return to her question.

'If you want me to tell you that old Hester was as mad as a rail louse then you are going to be disappointed,' Mark told her as he applied himself to his dessert. 'A little eccentric, maybe but . . . ' He tailed off with a shrug that told Clare he didn't intend to say much more.

'You are not very respectful. After all, she apparently brought you up.'

He shook his head slightly. 'My mother brought me up; Hester McMaster paid a lot of the bills. I suppose you think I should tug at my forelock and refer to her as Miss Hester, or even Miss McMaster, and call you ma'am, perhaps, while I'm about it?'

'Oh, don't be silly,' Clare muttered. 'Just tell me why she was so set on leaving everything to me.'

'Hasn't it crossed your mind that I may not know?'

'No,' Clare answered truthfully.

'Well, I'm sorry, but you'll just have to accept that. If you want to know any more go and ask Timothy Trimble. He was her lawyer — and before him his father was. If anyone knows anything about Miss Hester McMaster, then it will be our Timothy. After all, he drew up the will and presumably found you.'

'True,' Clare agreed. She pushed her empty bowl to one side and smiled. 'That was a lovely meal, Mark.'

He nodded, acknowledging her compliment. 'I try to please, ma'am,' he said facetiously, adding in his normal tone, 'coffee?' He got up to make it without waiting for her reply. 'Shall we take it outside?' he asked as he poured the boiling water on the grounds already in the plunger.

As she followed him out, Clare wondered what had happened to her interrogative skills which hitherto she had rather prided herself on as a lawyer. They drank their coffee in silence for a few moments, then she threw her key question at him. 'If, as you say, you don't know anything about anything — '

He interrupted her with a hand held high like a policeman on point duty. 'Correction. I never said I didn't know anything about anything — just that I had no idea what was going on in Miss Hester McMaster's mind.'

'Correction,' Clare conceded, 'but presumably you do know what is going on in your own mind, so why did you ask me here?'

'I thought it would be civil of me, and — '

'Oh, stop playing games!' Clare interrupted. 'Just tell me.'

'But I have told you.' He smiled blandly at her across the table. 'I thought I would like to know you better — and I thought you might enjoy it.'

'Hmmmph!' Clare resorted to a non-committal grunt, painfully aware that he was getting under her skin and that she was in real danger of losing her cool. The wretched man too often had this effect on her. She took a deep breath. 'I think' — she said, slowly and clearly — 'that you are being both flippant and obtuse. What was your real reason for asking me here? I'd like to know — but if you won't tell me then I shall just have to go back to Melbourne in ignorance.' As she spoke she placed her empty coffee cup down very deliberately in its saucer and, with her hands on the table, made to rise.

For a moment he stared back at her and

their gaze locked and held. When he spoke he was quite serious. 'I asked you because I thought that maybe we could put our heads together and perhaps work out some solution to what, on the face of it, seems an insolvable problem.'

Clare sat down again. 'You mean . . . the shop?'

He shrugged dismissively. 'That is only a small part of this unfortunate situation. I mean everything — your inheritance, this house, Boris, the shop. What are we going to do about it all?'

'As there is absolutely no way I can have that dog to live with me, it seems the only thing for me to do is to bow out gracefully.'

'Calling him 'that dog' doesn't make him any less of a problem or make him cease to exist. He is Boris,' Mark took her up somewhat testily.

'All right, Boris then.'

'What did you go to see Timothy about? Or more accurately, what did you hope he would do?'

'I wanted to see if there was any way I could sell part of this wretched legacy and just keep what I want,' Clare told him.

'And what is it that you particularly want?'

Clare shrugged. 'Well, this house, I suppose,' she admitted, adding in a rush, 'I can't really explain it — it's my dream house.'

'Maybe some memory stuck in your infantile brain.' He managed to make it sound as if he still thought her brain was infantile. Clare bridled, but before she could protest he went on, 'What about the business? Haven't you any interest in that?' Truthfully, Clare had almost forgotten about it during the course of her visit here. She hesitated before replying and he leaned towards her. With a new urgency, he asked her, 'Have you actually seen the will or are you just relying on what you have been told?'

'I — I — ' Clare stammered. Finally she shook her head. 'No, I haven't,' she admitted. 'Timothy wrote to me and asked me to come and see him. But no, I haven't actually seen a copy of the will.'

Mark startled her by leaning back in his chair with a great guffaw of derisive laughter. 'My God, Clare — and you call yourself a lawyer!'

'I only deal in divorce,' she said stiffly, trying not to squirm as she felt his amused gaze on her. 'Maybe I should go and see him again and ask to see it.'

'Maybe you should — but you don't have to.'

'Oh?'

'I have a copy.'

'Oh.' Clare, finding herself monosyllabic, forced herself to fill the silence with the question she knew he was waiting for. 'Can I see it?'

'But of course — if you have time. You were in a hurry to go a short while back.'

'I have time.' She kept her voice cool and level. This man was really the most maddening person she had ever met.

Mark got up and collected their coffee cups in silence. When Clare remained seated, he turned to her. 'I have it inside — come in if you want to see it, but I warn you, you may not like it.'

Clare was about to say 'Oh' yet again but bit off the monosyllable before she actually uttered it. She was discomfited to acknowledge how right Mark was. She had not behaved as she would expect anyone else to, let alone a lawyer. Inside the house Mark motioned her to a chair in the lounge room before disappearing into what she supposed was his bedroom and reappearing with a document tied with the legal pink tape that was so familiar to her. He undid it with what seemed like maddening slowness, unfolded it and ran his eyes over the wording before finally passing it over to her. Then he leaned back in his own chair to watch her reaction as she read.

Clare read through the document once fairly quickly then again much more slowly, a slight frown of bewilderment on her face. Finally she read it through yet again, then she let the hand holding it drop in her lap. 'But Mark — this isn't a bit like her will as Timothy Trimble explained it to me.'

'No? Tell me, Clare, just how did he explain it?'

Clare thought back, frowning slightly as she concentrated on remembering the exact wording of their conversation. 'He told me that I was the heir to my Aunt Hester McMaster's estate, but that there were certain conditions to be met if I was to inherit.'

'And you didn't actually see the will — or ask to see it?'

Clare shook her head. 'I just . . . believed him. After all . . . '

'He was a lawyer just like you — honour among lawyers just like among thieves?' Mark was sardonic.

'Well, yes, I suppose so. Anyway, I just believed him. Now I've read this I can see that was pretty foolish of me.'

'I'll say!'

'Well, now we have established my trusting innocence and stupidity to your satisfaction, perhaps we can move on and discuss this in a

116

little more depth,' Clare snapped. She didn't think she could bear the ill-concealed amusement on Mark's face much longer without losing her temper.

'You have read the last page?' Mark asked, suddenly intent.

Clare looked again at the document in her hand. There was a proviso to the effect that if she, Clare Davenport, was still unmarried within three months of her will being proved, then her estate was to be split. The shop was to go to Mark Fisk and the house to an animal charity that she was particularly interested in, with the proviso that Boris be cared for till his natural demise. Clare gaped. This was archaic, Victorian! How dare this mad old woman — who she didn't even remember — dictate to her how to run her life?

She slammed the papers down on the small coffee table between her and Mark and shot to her feet. 'That's it! You have your bloody shop and I'm off back to Melbourne!' she stormed.

She was already at the door when Mark's voice arrested her. 'There is a simple solution,' he told her. 'You could marry me!'

6

Clare stared at Mark, uncomfortably aware that she was looking unflatteringly stupefied. In fact, her mouth was actually hanging open. She snapped it shut, managed a weak half laugh and stood up. 'That is a preposterous idea, or would be if you meant it! But you are joking, of course.' This sounded even worse.

'Of course.' Mark's voice was frosty. 'And you are right, it is.' Clare looked up and met his eyes: they were worse than frosty, they were glacial. His mouth, once so sweet, was tight and thin and set in a hard line. They stared at one another for what seemed an uncomfortable length of time; Clare was the first to turn away.

'Thank you for the meal,' she mumbled as she moved to the door, feeling in her bag for her car keys.

'Don't mention it.' His voice was as polite and distant as hers as he stepped forward and opened the door for her. 'When do you go back to Melbourne?' He sounded totally disinterested, like some bored host glad to see an unwelcome visitor depart and making conversation merely to fill silence.

'Tomorrow.' Clare's tone was brusque.

'Then I'll say goodbye and have a good journey.'

'Thanks — ' Clare began, but before she could bid him good night the door closed in her face.

She stared at it for a moment then turned abruptly on her heel and marched to her car, muttering to herself, 'Well, of all the rude so and sos.' Adding, as she dropped into the driving seat and fitted her key in the ignition, 'Marry him indeed. Not likely — not if he was the last man on earth.'

She ground the gears painfully and her tyres scrunched on the gravel at the side of the road as she drove away. She was halfway back to Castlemaine and her motel before she was calm enough to ask herself just why she was so uptight about his proposal, if that was what it really was. And if it wasn't, why should his misguided sense of humour upset her so much? She was not yet willing to accept the idea that she might be offended because he hadn't really meant it.

Too uptight to sleep, she flicked on the TV in her room. There was nothing that grabbed her attention but the voice emanating from it was better than silence, so she left it on as she gathered up her clothes and stowed them into her case ready to leave early in the morning.

But after a restless night she decided that she needed to know more about this mysterious aunt of hers. As it was she wasn't even sure whether the relationship was on her mother or father's side. She would go to see Timothy Trimble before she left, and that of course meant she had to wait until his office opened; even later if he couldn't see her straight away.

He couldn't — she had to wait till ten o'clock. The need to talk to someone was so strong that she almost dialled Robert's office. Over the last year or so she had talked over so many problems with him and believed him to be the fount of wisdom, at least in the early days of their relationship. Not so much lately, she admitted to herself. All the same, it would be good to talk to someone. Her hand was actually hovering over the handset when it rang, startling her into picking it up without thought. She was startled to hear Mark's voice, cool and rather distant.

'I guess I owe you an apology, Clare.' He spoke stiffly. 'I guess the wine was stronger than I thought or I drank too much of it. I wouldn't like to think you left this part of the world harbouring ill-feeling or thinking I held any for you.'

'Thank you,' Clare mumbled, adding, 'I feel that I owe you an apology too. I am afraid

I was very rude and — and ungracious.' She didn't find it easy to admit to her own faults and was afraid there was a grudging note in her voice. She thought he must have detected it too for after a pause he said simply, 'No hard feelings, then?'

'None,' she agreed.

'Then I'll say goodbye again. Goodbye, Clare, it was nice knowing you.'

'Goodbye.' She replaced the receiver slowly after hearing what seemed like a click of finality as he replaced his. He had sounded as if this really was the end of — what? Well, she wouldn't be helping him any more in the shop, that was certain. She was surprised at the real pang that thought gave her. She had done it in the first place out of simple curiosity, to find out just what sort of a business it was. She had remained because it represented a challenge and, rather to her surprise, she had actually enjoyed it. She refused to acknowledge, even to herself, that she had enjoyed Mark's company. She wondered what would happen to it now. She failed to see how it could become a viable business or even survive without an injection of capital.

She collected the last of her possessions and took her cases out to her car, settled her account and then made her way to Timothy's office. She was kept waiting and wondered whether this was genuine or whether he was playing power games with her. By the time she was eventually sent in she was feeling cross and out of sorts — cross, she told herself, with Timothy, not out of sorts because for some reason she was feeling down in the mouth at the end to her little break. A break which, she felt now, had been a mistake to take at all and had turned into a miserable failure.

Timothy rose to his feet to greet her and extended his hand over the desk. She took it after a brief hesitation before sitting down opposite him.

'Miss Davenport .. er . . . Clare, how nice to see you before you leave.' Clare winced at what she felt was a palpably insincere remark on his part. 'What can I do for you?' Before she could answer he shrugged slightly and lifted his hands in a gesture indicating that he was actually helpless to do anything.

Clare forced herself to smile but her voice was firm as she answered. 'I would like a copy of my aunt's will, please.' She had braced herself for a refusal but was surprised to see him visibly relax.

'But of course, Clare, you should have a copy — what an oversight that you have not. I will get one for you. Bear with me a moment.' He got up and left the room, returning a few moments later with a folded and tape-tied document which he handed to her with a slight smile. 'But I am afraid there is little I can do — I wish I could help you, believe me I do.'

Clare thought his protestations were a little overdone then immediately chided herself for being suspicious and cynical. 'I am aware of that,' she assured him. 'I just felt I would like a copy for myself. After all, she does seem to have been about my only living relative.' As she said the words the incongruity of the statement struck her: whatever Hester McMaster had been, she was not now a living relative. There was a faint smile curving her lips as she stood up and held out her hand once more to Timothy.

'I'll say goodbye then, and — thank you.' Even as she spoke she wondered just what she was actually thanking him for.

He took her hand. 'Goodbye . . . Clare.' There was that slight hesitation before her name. 'I am really sorry I couldn't be of more help to you but if at any time you feel I can — well, you have my phone number.'

'Yes,' she answered vaguely and turned towards the door. Her hand was actually on the knob when she turned back to face him again. He was staring after her with an expression she could not fathom. 'There is just one thing I would like to know. Just how was Hester McMaster related to me? I mean, was it through my father or my mother?'

For a second he looked nonplussed. 'Why, your father, of course. Surely you knew that?'

Clare shook her head. 'No, in fact I can't remember ever hearing about her existence until I received your letter.' She closed the door firmly behind her and with a brief nod at the girl at the reception desk strode outside. She tossed the will on to the passenger seat with her handbag, turned the key in the ignition and headed for Melbourne. She had been driving for barely ten minutes and the outskirts of Castlemaine were only just behind her when she wondered how Timothy Trimble had known she was leaving the district. She had barely known herself until last night. She was convinced she hadn't mentioned it when she rang his office to make an appointment. Could Mark have told him? And if so, why?

She was tempted to pull in at the first wayside parking bay she came to and call Mark on her mobile. But what was the point? She *was* leaving — she had finished with the whole business. She was heading back to Melbourne, her flat, her job and her normal life. Her thoughts slid to Robert — a week or two ago she would have included him in this, but now she was not sure whether she wanted to ever see him again. Damn all men, she thought and switched the radio on rather louder than necessary to drown out the sound of her own thoughts.

* * *

Clare's eyes were drawn from habit to the answer machine as she let herself into her flat. The light was flicking. There were a couple of irritating non-messages. How she hated those: surely if anyone bothered to dial her number they could leave some sort of message, or did they enjoy the thought that she would be left wondering who it was? Probably, she decided, as Robert's voice came on.

'Clare — are you back?' (of course she was or she would not be hearing this, she thought irritably.) 'I'm sorry about the other night — I guess I shouldn't have descended on you without warning. Call me back please some time.' How uncharacteristic of Robert to apologize, she reflected, but since he had — and she had, it seemed, scuttled all other possibilities — she might as well. She dialled his number at his office without stopping to ask herself just what she meant by 'other possibilities'.

'Clare.' Robert's voice was guarded and she guessed there was someone in his office, then he said, 'Clare', in a totally different voice and she could almost see his secretary discreetly closing the door behind herself. 'You are back then?'

'Yes,' she said shortly, once more marvelling at his ability to state the obvious but biting off any comment. 'I got your message.'

'Look, I'm free this evening — how about dinner?'

'I really don't think . . . ' Here they were back in the old routine. What had happened to her decision to make a clean break?

'Of course, if you're tired — or busy — but I would like to see you.' He hesitated then continued, 'I need to see you. I — have to talk to you.'

'All right,' Clare capitulated, aware that she sounded far from gracious, which she felt was unfair of her as Robert was almost grovelling. Well, perhaps that was a little strong but she had not heard him almost beg her like this before. To her chagrin, she realized that was more often her role. They arranged a time and a place and hung off. Clare flung her case down on the bed and prowled round her flat trying to make it fit her, or to fit herself into it, as she had before she left five days ago. She put her clothes away, then made herself a cup of coffee; she was hungry but after a week away from home her fridge was, like Mother Hubbard's cupboard, extremely bare. She found some crackers and a bit of stale cheese and ate them. She should, she knew, go out and buy some basic supplies — bread and milk at the very least — but she seemed gripped by an odd inertia. For some reason she was unable to pinpoint, her flat no longer felt like home, or at least not as much as it had when she left it barely a week ago. The motel room certainly had not filled that category so what was she thinking of? Stupid to ask that, she told herself, when the image of an old stone cottage swam into her consciousness.

She was being utterly ridiculous, verging on the neurotic. It was time to take control of her wayward thoughts, get back into her real life, get her act together. On the wave of this pep talk to herself, she snatched up her purse and headed off for the nearest store.

★   ★   ★

She noticed the difference in Robert as soon as he picked her up; it was hard to pinpoint exactly what it was, but his behaviour towards her reminded her of the early days of their relationship, before they sank into the apathy of familiarity.

He was solicitous in opening doors for her, and in the restaurant he consulted her about the menu. Maybe a break was a good thing now and then, Clare thought. She looked up at him when she had made her selection; he was looking at her anxiously, at the same time fiddling with the cutlery. He was not behaving like Robert at all.

'Is something the matter?' she asked.

'No, not really — not really the matter,' he hedged.

Clare shrugged. 'Either there is or there isn't,' she found herself snapping. 'If there is tell me about it, if there isn't then lighten up.' She was aware that he was staring at her in some discomfort and hurriedly began to apologize. 'I'm sorry, Robert — I guess I'm feeling out of sorts, tired after the trip back and . . . well, one way and another the week wasn't too successful.'

'I'm sorry to hear that . . . ' He reached across the table for her hand, but she slid it away unobtrusively before his fingers touched her. 'I hope, well, had hoped, that what I have to ask you would please you. Clare, will you marry me?'

'Marry you? But you can't — you're already married!' Clare spluttered. What wouldn't she have given to hear those words a few months back? Now all she could do was stare at him in a sort of stupefied amazement.

He reached across the white cloth again and this time managed to pin her hand beneath his own. 'You were absolutely right to behave as you did when I landed on you like that at your motel — absolutely — and I'm glad you did because you forced me to see sense. Linda and I have parted and I am asking you in all sincerity to marry me as soon as our divorce becomes absolute.'

Clare stared at him. Where was the catch in her breath, the euphoria that she should be feeling, and would have felt only a short time ago?

'I — I don't know what to say . . . ' she finally stammered with absolute truth.

'There is only one thing you need say,' Robert retorted with a sort of arch gallantry that Clare would have thought quite alien to him.

'But Robert . . . ' She was about to add facetiously, 'This is so sudden,' before she remembered humour was not always his strong point, especially if he thought it was being directed at himself.

'You don't have to answer immediately. Tell me about your trip — this inheritance of yours. What exactly do you get?'

Clare shrugged. 'Absolutely nothing as far as I can make out,' she told him, smiling at the waitress who had just arrived with their meal.

'Nothing? What do you mean? I thought you were the only surviving relative of the old girl? Do you mean that by the time all just due debts and all that are paid off there will be very little left?'

'Nope, that's not what I mean. I mean I get nothing.'

'Then the whole trip was a total waste of time.'

'You could say that . . . ' Clare began, then she thought of her time there. She thought, infuriatingly, of startling blue eyes, and she knew that whatever else the trip had been it was not a total waste of time. 'You could say that,' she repeated, 'but I wouldn't. I learned a lot — I saw a part of Victoria I really didn't know at all and I met some nice people.' What an inadequate word that was, she thought, and amended it to 'some interesting people'.

'Such as the character I saw when I turned up there?'

Clare looked him in the eye. 'Yes — such as Timothy Trimble,' she told him blandly. 'The lawyer looking after my aunt's estate.' Let Robert think what he liked, draw whatever conclusions he pleased; it let her off the hook of having to explain Mark and Flowers For the Journey and the time she had spent helping him, none of which he would understand in the slightest. In fact, looking back she couldn't really understand herself, and why she had cared so much for the future, or non-future, of a run-down little shop in a small provincial town.

'Tell me why there is no inheritance.'

'Tell me why you were so anxious to see me tonight,' Clare countered. 'Had you a special reason or are you just a glutton for punishment, a total masochist, after the way I treated you last time we met?'

Robert shrugged. 'Let's forget that, shall we? It was an unfortunate occurrence. Neither of us I feel behaved particularly well.'

Clare smiled. 'Fair enough,' she agreed. If he was prepared to take that line then surely she, in all conscience, had to meet him halfway. 'Now tell me why, after so long, have you suddenly asked me to marry you?' She felt little more than idle curiosity and wondered how long it would be before the ecstatic delight she should be feeling began to kick in. 'Has Linda walked out on you or something?'

'Yes — no — no.'

Clare looked up from her food in surprise

at this very odd reply. 'She has.' It was a statement, not a question, and it was the look of total confusion and utter embarrassment on his face that told her. It was a look she had not only never seen on Robert's face before but moreover would never have associated with him. One of the things about him that she had always found so attractive was the fact that he was, or so it seemed to her, always in command, both of himself and circumstances. Conversely it was this very quality that had caused her so much pain over the time she had known him. She had simply been unable to accept that if he had truly wanted to marry her, he could have done.

'She has, hasn't she?' she demanded now.

'Well, yes, she has. But it's not like you think. We — we had a talk and we agreed to part. It seems that Linda has, well, someone else in her life.'

'And what about Annabel?' After all she, not Linda, had been the main excuse, or reason, that Robert had always given to remain in his marriage.

'Annabel is old enough now to fend for herself.'

'Yes,' was all Clare could think of to say. 'So now you are free you want to marry me, is that right?'

'That's what I've been telling you. So will you, Clare?'

Clare shook her head. 'I don't think so, Robert.' She almost laughed aloud at the expression of comic astonishment on his face.

'But Clare, darling, it's what we've dreamed of for years.'

'Have we? Have you — or just me?'

'Is there someone else?' Robert's voice was sharp.

Clare shook her head. 'Nope,' she said succinctly. 'It's just that . . . oh, I don't know, Robert. I guess it's just that I feel you — we — have missed the boat somehow.'

He leaned across the table and placed his hand on her arm. 'Give it a try — please, Clare.'

She looked up and met his eyes, kind grey eyes. He was a good kind man, wasn't he? She should know — she had known him intimately now for two years, and he was offering her what she had yearned for most of that time? Why wasn't she over the moon? There was — as she had assured him — no one else. She sighed, and when he begged her once more to give it a go, found herself murmuring, 'I'll think about it, Robert, I really will. It's just that . . . '

'That's good enough for me — for the moment. Now tell me about your trip to

133

Castlemaine. Explain about this legacy that apparently isn't.'

'Well,' Clare began, 'it seems that my aunt had a dog. She was extremely attached to him, and there is this clause in her will that her heir must take on the dog and give it a home for the rest of its life — '

'Or they don't get anything. But that's absurd — quite absurd!' Robert interrupted. 'What that means is that she has actually left her estate to a dog.' He managed to invest so much scorn in the last word that Clare, remembering beautiful and dignified Boris, almost protested. 'I'm not even sure that is legal. But if it is you could contest the will. Or . . . ' He paused and looked at her. 'You could adopt this little dog — what is it, a peke, a poodle, pomeranian, something like that?'

Clare smiled both at his unconscious alliteration and the picture of Boris she still held in her mind. 'Hardly — he is actually a borzoi, a Russian wolfhound. Very large. He would barely fit into my flat, even if I were allowed to have a dog there.'

7

Clare stirred and turned over, rousing herself from sleep. As she did she felt another body close to her own. Her first reaction was panic. Then she remembered, Robert had come home with her the previous evening. She moved slightly to her side of the bed so that their bodies no longer touched. How had this happened? More accurately, how had she let this happen? Hadn't she made a decision to end this relationship when she celebrated her thirtieth birthday — alone? She had — so what was Robert doing in her bed?

Wide awake, she swung her legs cautiously over the side of the bed and slid her feet into her slippers. She stole out and closed the door between the bedroom and the rest of the flat, then switched on the electric jug. While she waited for it to boil she dropped a tea bag into a mug and sat down on one of the two bar stools alongside the tiny breakfast bench. Once made she held the hot tea between her hands and sniffed the steam appreciatively before taking a tentative sip. How, she wondered, was she going to get out of this. Why had she ever been such an idiot as to let him into her flat and her bed? The answer, she reflected gloomily, was probably too much wine and a guilty conscience. Guilty not because of her two-year relationship with him but because when she had woken up on her thirtieth birthday to the realization that she was travelling a road that led nowhere she had not been explicit enough in making her feelings clear to Robert. The trouble was he was really so nice, usually so kind; and now circumstances had altered everything so that he could offer her the things she thought she wanted. The security of marriage, children of her own before her biological clock ran out; the big problem was that now he was available she wasn't at all sure that she wanted these things. But how could she explain all that to him without hurting him?

'I guess,' she said out loud, 'I'd better accept what I'm being offered.' She had wished for it long enough and now it seemed it was hers for the taking. *Be careful what you wish, in case you get it!* Who had once said that to her? She couldn't remember. Anyway, it was a ridiculous sentiment — didn't we all hope for our wishes and dreams to come true? She got up, put her cup in the sink and returned to bed.

★ ★ ★

'You haven't said much about the week you spent in Castlemaine.' Robert sounded disgruntled, or maybe it was because he was speaking through a mouthful of cornflakes. Clare repressed a smile as a couplet she had recently read somewhere flashed into her mind and struck her with its aptness.

*The glances over cocktails that seemed
   so very sweet
Don't seem quite so amorous over the
   Shredded Wheat*

Robert, she knew, would not see any humour in it.

'There's not much to tell.' Clare sounded casual, almost offhand, as she pulled the coffee pot towards her. 'What do you want to know, anyway?'

'Well, more about this inheritance of yours, for a start. I don't accept the absurd reason you gave me for not accepting it.'

'Absurd or not, it's the truth. And why bother discussing it if it doesn't exist — as far as I am concerned anyway.'

'Why don't you get someone from your firm on to it? I wouldn't trust that solicitor fellow up there, anyway.'

Clare suppressed a smile. No, she thought, you wouldn't: your meeting with him was not exactly conducive to trust and amiability. But she said nothing.

'There must be someone in the mob you work with who handles this sort of thing. You shouldn't let it go unchallenged — fight it. She had no other relatives — there's probably quite a tidy inheritance there.'

'Her house, her business and her dog,' Clare was stung into retorting.

'Business — what sort of business?'

'A run-down flower shop — more of a liability than an asset.' Clare jumped down from her stool, 'I have to get dressed. I — I need to go into the office.'

'But it's Saturday — you don't have to be in till Monday. You took time off, remember.'

'I know but — well there is something I want to do. I need to go in — just for a short while.' She turned and looked back at him from the bedroom door and wondered how on earth she was going to be able to face him at breakfast every morning for the rest of her life.

When she came out of the shower, Robert was gone. She was dressed for the office but now she was alone the need to go there had dissipated. She picked up her phone and dialled Zoe's home number.

She had to be fetched to the phone by her husband and when she came on the line she sounded faintly breathless and spoke against the background noises of Saturday morning family life. Clare almost hung up, it was hardly fair to call at the weekend.

'Clare, where are you? Is everything all right?' Zoe's concern stabbed her conscience.

'I'm fine — and I'm home . . . '

'Then . . . ?' The question hovered between them. Clare so seldom called her after work hours as she felt it was unfair of her to encroach on her friend's family time.

'I — I just wondered — that is, if you aren't tied up too much. I wondered . . . could you meet me for a coffee?'

'I have to take the kids to tennis,' Zoe hedged, 'but I don't really have to stay there. I can drop them off at the courts and meet you for an hour . . . '

'Can I meet you at the tennis club, sit with you while they play?' Clare suggested. She knew that Zoe liked to be there for them and they liked her there.

* * *

'Come on — tell all. I know you haven't suddenly had a burning desire to watch children knocking a ball back and forth,' Zoe said when they had been seated side by side on a wooden bench listening to the not too steady twang of rubber on racket without speaking.

'I went out with Robert last night — he spent the night with me. He says he is getting a divorce.'

'So why the lack of enthusiasm? Isn't that what you have wanted for so long?' Zoe looked at her friend in genuine puzzlement.

'Yes but . . . '

Zoe turned and looked at her keenly. 'But that was before you went to Castlemaine. Is that what you were going to say?'

Clare gasped. 'Yes — no — that had nothing to do with it. I decided, more or less, that I wasn't entirely sure I really wanted to continue with him before I went. Going up there had no bearing on things at all.'

'So?' Zoe raised a cynical eyebrow. 'Why did you sleep with him last night?'

'Oh, I don't know — it was a mistake. It just got me in deeper. He asked me out to dinner and told me he and Linda have split up — he really does want to marry me, I think. I have wished for it so long. It seemed . . . well, unfair to him somehow, to say I had changed my mind now it was suddenly possible.'

Zoe grinned. 'What have I always told you? Be careful what you wish for . . . '

'I know, I know. In case you get it,' Clare interrupted.

Zoe considered her friend; she had known Clare so long that she was certain there was more behind this sudden indecision than an attack of cold feet. 'Maybe . . . ' she said thoughtfully, 'maybe you should go back to Castlemaine. Finish your unfinished business there before you make a decision.'

Clare didn't answer immediately. Zoe watched her mouth set in a mutinous line and noted with wry amusement the slight flush staining her throat but when she spoke it was only to say in a cool voice, 'Unfinished business?' She turned and looked her friend squarely in the eye. 'I don't know what you mean — I did everything I had to do there.'

'Which was?'

'I saw the lawyer and discovered the whole thing had been some sort of bizarre mistake: apparently I am not in any way connected to this Hester McMaster, so the will and her estate are nothing to do with me.' Even as she spoke Clare wondered why she wasn't telling Zoe the truth. She was, after all, her oldest friend, her greatest, her only confidante. Which was why she had asked her to meet her this morning.

'I . . . see,' Zoe said slowly, though in all honestly she didn't. What she was certain of

141

was that there was something she was not being told. 'If you wanted my approval — '

'Of course I don't want your approval — what a ridiculous idea.'

'Well, if you want me to tell you whether or not you should regularize your relationship with Robert by tying the knot then I'm not going to do that either.'

'I don't want you to *tell* me anything. I suppose' — Clare lifted her shoulders slightly in the barest of shrugs — 'I suppose what I really need is a sounding board.'

'Go ahead then — talk.' Zoe looked at her watch. 'You have about thirty-seven minutes before we are surrounded by noisy kids.'

Clare frowned, searching for the right words to begin, so absorbed in her own thoughts she missed the touch of impatience in Zoe's voice.

'You are quite right,' she said at last. 'of course this is what I have wanted ever since I first met Robert. Well not quite then but certainly since I . . . since we . . . well, once I knew how he felt about me.'

She paused and Zoe cut in. 'Since you first started sleeping with him and gave up dating other men.'

'Well, yes — I suppose so.' Clare thought she wouldn't have put it quite like that but had to admit the truth of the statement.

142

'Now, I'm suddenly not so sure.'

'A bit late in the day to find out, if you ask me, but I suppose better late than never,' Zoe remarked drily, her head going from side to side as she followed the game in front of her. Fond as she was of Clare, she had never thought her involvement with Robert such a good idea and had never believed for an instant that the day would ever dawn when marriage would be on the cards. Clare, she thought, was wasting her life. Well, it seemed she had been wrong. But why on earth was she in such a fizz now things seemed to be going her way?

'I read somewhere ... ' Clare smiled slightly when Zoe said this. She had often remarked that her friend's mind was like an untidy desk, full of irrelevant bits of information, which were usually produced with the preface of either 'I read somewhere' or 'I heard somewhere'. 'I don't know where but I am sure I read somewhere that relationships tend to break up after a certain period of time, irrespective of whether the couple involved are married.' When Clare's only response was a vague 'Hmmmm', which could have meant anything, she continued, 'What brought all this up, anyway? I mean, how come Robert suddenly finds he is not as much married as he would have had you believe? How is it that all of a sudden he is free?'

'Well, he always said when Annabel was older — and anyway, it seems Linda wants out.'

Zoe gave a sardonic grunt. 'So, Linda wants out — well, that's not surprising — but do you want in?'

'Oh, hell, Zoe! I just don't know, I really don't know. But I feel so bad turning round and saying I don't want Robert just when he is free after all these years.'

'You feel bad! Get real, Clare — he's strung you along for two years and now because he thinks he might lose you altogether he suddenly says, 'Let's get married.' I don't know what you are agonizing about: when he let you down on your birthday you were ready to give him the flick, now, all of a sudden you're sorry for him and thinking about tying yourself to him for the rest of your life. Surely in your daily work you see enough marriage failures and mismatches to convince you that feeling sorry for someone, feeling guilty about them, is not a basis for a good marriage.'

'I didn't say anything about either feeling guilty or sorry for him.'

'Not in so many words — no — but you certainly implied it and one thing you didn't mention was love.'

Clare jumped abruptly to her feet. 'I came to talk to you as a friend — if I need a counsellor I'll go to one.' With a curt, 'See you in the office Monday,' she turned on her heel and walked away without a backward glance.

Zoe watched her go, let out her breath in a slight sigh more of exasperation than anything, shrugged, and gave her undivided attention to her children playing tennis.

It took Clare twenty minutes to walk briskly back to her flat, and by the time she arrived much of her anger at Zoe had abated. It was herself she was annoyed with. What on earth was wrong with her? She had got what she had wanted, hadn't she? Robert was prepared to commit to her. Even as she thought this, the rebel idea flashed into her mind that total commitment from Robert was not what she wanted. She stopped short of asking herself whether Robert himself was the problem.

'I'm just sick of being 'the other woman',' she told herself out loud as she made herself a cup of coffee. Even as she spoke she remembered saying this once to Robert, and his reply, 'You are not the other woman, you are *the* woman.' It had touched her and mollified her at the time, but now she thought, what utter crap. A typical example of men lying and women believing them.

She slumped down in her most comfortable armchair with her coffee; maybe a mild caffeine fix would help cure her disgruntled mood. Perhaps she was just jaded; she had been dealing with other people's marital messes too long. Immersed in her thoughts, she jumped so much when her phone rang that she almost spilt her coffee. For a moment she let it ring, waiting for the answering service to click in; she had put it on when she went out earlier and left it on when she returned. The voice that suddenly answered her own message did make her jump enough to slop a drop of scalding coffee on to her hand. She put down the mug and jumped to her feet. Snatching up the phone, she cut in while the voice was still speaking.

She regretted her impulsive action immediately and stared at the receiver in her hand, wondering what lunacy had made her do this and why she found it hard to speak now she had.

'Hello.' Her voice came out as something midway between a whisper and a squeak, so she cleared her throat and began again. 'Hello, Mark.'

'Clare, is that you? Of course it is — you've just said so. I was just about to put the phone down. I thought either I had the wrong number or there was something wrong with your answering service.'

'It's me.' She waited for him to tell her why he had rung, but when he didn't she asked, 'What are you ringing for?' Then another thought struck her. 'How did you get my phone number?'

'You left a little address book behind full of phone numbers, even your own. I thought you might want it back.'

'Thanks.' Trying to sound casual, Clare was afraid she merely sounded offhand — almost rude. 'Thanks very much.' Surely she hadn't put her own number in that little pocket directory?

'Your number and address were inside the cover,' Mark told her, almost as if she had spoken her thoughts out loud.

'Oh. Well, thanks very much for letting me know it's safe — I would have been mad when I discovered it missing. Could you mail it to me?'

'I can do better than that, I can deliver it in person. I'm — '

'No, don't bother — just mail it,' Clare cut in swiftly.

'No bother, no bother at all,' Mark told her blithely. 'See you in five minutes.'

'No!' Clare protested, then stared at the

handset burring in her fingers. He had rung off. There was no way she could avoid seeing him, unless she was very quick in making her escape. She slowly replaced the phone, wondering why she was being so absurd. He was obviously here in Melbourne for some reason and was kindly returning her property, left behind, presumably in Flowers For The Journey. She would just open the door and receive it politely, then equally politely bid him goodbye and close it again.

She went quickly to her bedroom, ran a comb through her hair, touched up her light make-up and, almost as an afterthought, sprayed herself with perfume. As she turned away from the mirror, the doorbell pealed.

'Hello — thank you.' She reached out for the little notebook in his hand. 'You shouldn't have bothered,' was what she intended to say, but somehow after they had stared at one another for what seemed a very long few seconds, she heard herself saying instead, 'Come in,' as she stepped back allowing him to pass her.

'I — I was just having a cup of coffee. Would you like one?'

'Love one.' He followed her into the microscopic kitchen area, filling it entirely, it seemed to Clare, who felt suddenly breathless.

Mark looked round with interest and, it seemed to her, amusement, while she got out another mug and busied herself being the hostess.

'You were right, of course,' he told her. 'Boris would be a bit large in here, or should I say this place would be a bit small for Boris?'

'I'm glad you see my point,' Clare said drily as she placed the two mugs of coffee on a small tray and led the way through to the lounge-cum-living room. 'Make yourself at home,' she told him, indicating the sofa on the opposite side of the room to the chair she sat in herself. The coffee was too hot to drink, so for what seemed an age they sat in silence occasionally taking a tentative and hopeful sip. When they spoke it was in unison.

'Who is in the shop today?' Clare asked.

'Why did you leave in such a rush?' Mark wanted to know. 'And why were you so mad?'

They shrugged and smiled at each other; it was an odd little moment of intimacy and understanding. It surprised Clare, leaving her temporarily bereft of words so that it was Mark who answered her question first.

'No one — it's closed.'

'Oh. Can you afford to do that?' Clare ignored his original question.

'Nope — but neither can I afford to pay

anyone to mind it.'

'Oh.' Clare wished she could stop saying that. 'What have you come up to Melbourne for? No — sorry — I don't mean to put you through the third degree, and it's no business of mine, anyway.'

'It is, because you are the reason I am here — like I told you, I came to return your belongings.'

'But you can't possibly have come all this way just to give me back that little book which you could quite easily have put in an envelope and mailed to me,' Clare protested.

'I came to see if you had given any consideration to my proposal yet?'

'Proposal?' Clare stared blankly at Mark, wondering whether she was being very obtuse or had missed something along the way.

'You have a very short memory. Or a very selective one — what your Aunt Hester used to refer to as 'a good forgettery'.'

Clare smiled at the small joke but when she looked across at Mark his face was impassive and his eyes cold when they met hers.

'I asked you to marry me, Ms Clare Davenport. I suggested it as a way round this impasse we seem to be in.'

She looked straight back. 'But that would be very foolish on your part. If I don't take up this inheritance you get the shop. The rest, undoubtedly the better part, goes to Boris, correct?'

'Correct,' he agreed, 'but if you married me, and naturally I should expect my wife to live with me, we could live in the cottage, with Boris, and combine our not inconsiderable talents to turn Flowers For The Journey into the trendy — and profitable — little business it should be.'

'We could,' she agreed, 'if I married you, but that would involve giving up my quite lucrative career here in Melbourne and relocating. There is also another slight problem.'

'Which is?'

'*Who* is . . . ' Clare corrected him. 'Robert, my fiancé, the man I am going to marry.'

'I know what a fiancé is,' Mark rapped, 'but I wasn't aware you had one. Since when, may I ask?'

'Since yesterday — well, for years, actually.' She felt herself flushing, whether at the patent incompatibility of these two statements or because Mark seemed to be holding her with his gaze. Before she managed to tear her eyes away from his face, she saw his eyebrows shoot up in skeptical query.

'Have I missed something or are we just playing a game of true or false here?'

'Neither. I have known Robert for over two

151

years. He asked me to marry him yesterday.'

'And you, I presume, said yes. Should be a safe if dull ride — no one could accuse the guy of being impulsive, could they?' Clare did not miss the mocking twist to his mouth. She looked away, not just embarrassed now but oddly ashamed, as if she had done something unforgivably stupid.

'He the one who came chasing up to Castlemaine to see what you were up to?' Before she could reply, Clare felt her upper arms gripped and she was turned round, none too gently, so that she was more or less forced to look Mark in the face.

'You are hurting me,' she said feebly. He was, but she didn't really mind; there was an odd but quite exquisite sensation flowing from his hands to her skin, causing it to throb and burn beneath his touch. He didn't let go.

'Before you give him your final answer, come back once more and see what could be yours.' He pulled her roughly close to him and before she realized his intention, bent and kissed her on the mouth. Startled and unexpectedly aroused, Clare's lips parted involuntarily and she allowed his probing tongue to search out hers. For a moment she kissed him back, then pushed away. His hands dropped abruptly to his sides and Clare realized that he had virtually been supporting her as she staggered slightly. 'You'll come.' It was a statement, not a question, and he turned swiftly to the door so that he did not see Clare shaking her head.

He turned at the door and with a grin, just as if there had been no passion a second or so ago, said, 'Tell that would-be fiancé of yours that you need time to think about it — a couple of years at least!'

'Fiancé, not would-be fiancé,' Clare protested but found she was only grumbling to empty air. Mark had gone, leaving her feeling strangely bereft and the small flat empty and hollow.

How absurd, Clare thought. 'How ridiculous to think she would go chasing up to Castlemaine again — ever,' she said aloud to herself, the words echoing back to her, or so it seemed. All the same Mark had planted a seed in her mind that seemed determined to sprout, however much she tried to kill it.

Clare heated up the coffee and poured herself another cup in the hope that it would encourage her brain, rather than her physical sense, to work. She sat down and cradled the warm cup in her hands, her features creasing as she strove to remember the exact wording of her aunt's will. What was it in that absurd codicil? Something about her being married within a certain length of time of the will being proved, otherwise she lost all claims. It was ridiculous, quite archaic. All the same, was that the reason, the only reason, that Mark had asked her to marry him? The thought was deflating. At least Robert had no nefarious reason to want to marry her. He had no idea of the exact contents of the will. If she failed to inherit, Mark received the shop anyway, but he probably felt that was a liability rather than an asset. It was quite clear that he had asked her to get hold of the house — after all, he was very comfortably ensconced there, and she could appreciate it would be a wrench to let it go. She had never owned it, just had it dangled tantalizingly in front of her, and even she felt a pang. She thought she liked it so much because it fitted so well her mental dream house. Now she wondered if it was possible that it was her dream house because she had within her a buried memory of visiting it as a very young child.

She wished she could really remember it. It must have been one of the few times she had actually been taken anywhere by both parents. They had separated when she was only two years old. Her father had returned to England and only came back to Australia to 'claim' her when her mother died. Clare sometimes thought bitterly that her mother had only had time to bother with her in the spells between the men that she made Clare call 'uncle'. She had learned to be on her own and to see scholastic achievement as a way out. Her father encouraged this, seeing in Clare the fulfilment of his own thwarted ambition. He had been pleased when she got into college and when she chose law had felt he had done his duty by her; she would now be financially secure. Maybe it was because he felt he had done his duty by her that he succumbed to the cancer that slowly destroyed him. Clare, more out of gratitude and tepid affection than real love, had cared for him till he died, feeling guilty because she didn't feel more and sometimes angry with him for not fighting back. The main fabric of their relationship seemed to be duty, yet now and then she caught a glimpse of the father she remembered from her very early child-hood and as she grew older wondered what had happened to turn him into the quiet almost defeated man she knew.

Her thoughts turned to Robert. After all, as she had been at pains to point out to Mark, he was her fiancé. She would ask his advice about this odd inheritance.

She broached the subject over dinner that evening. The memory of their last uncomfort-able meal together hung between them rather like a wraith. Both, Clare thought, were being careful not to mention anything that might bring that back to mind.

Clare straightened her cutlery for the umpteenth time, sliding it out of place and back again on the smooth damask white cloth in the very upmarket restaurant Robert had chosen for what he obviously considered was a special dinner. 'Robert . . . '

'Yes?' He raised his eyes to her face. He had been following her nervous movements, wondering what was wrong with her. Were they the prelude to some sort of outburst? He hoped not; he did so dislike scenes in public places.

'Robert, I was wondering if you could help me?'

'Of course, any way I can, you know that.' He meant to sound soothing and helpful, but Clare thought he was unctious.

'Could you — would you help me over this inheritance, or as it seems at the moment, non-inheritance? If you saw the will — talked to Timothy Trimble — you might be able to sort something out.' Even as she spoke Clare thought that 'sorting something out' might just produce more problems. She shrugged deprecatingly. Perhaps not — probably better just to let things go. After all, what on earth would she do with a property as far away as

Maldon? She wished she had not broached the subject.

'But of course I will — let me have a look at it and I'll do anything I can to help you. From what you've told me, it does seem as if you're not being treated at all as you should be.'

'Oh, I can't really complain. Everyone has been most helpful — it's just that . . . ' She trailed off. Just what? And why had she stopped short of mentioning the shop? She shrugged again and smiled at Robert across the table. 'I don't really think it is worth bothering about. After all, it isn't much. Probably more bother than it's worth.'

'Let me see the will, then I'll tell you if anything can be done.'

'Well, I — I don't actually have a copy of it,' Clare lied, remembering the ridiculous codicil and wishing with all her heart she had never broached the subject. Better still never heard about Aunt Hester, her will, her dog, her house and her business. Without them she would probably have been joyfully planning her wedding to Robert now. They had disrupted the whole even tenor of her life. She looked up to see that Robert was looking at her over the plate of food that had just been placed in front of him with amazement. His mouth, she noted, was very slightly open

157

and his eyes were almost popping. She had an absurd desire to giggle but dropped her eyes to her own plate and merely felt almost as foolish as she was sure he considered her.

'Not got a copy!' He sounded aghast but quickly brightened. 'Ah well, not to worry,' he assured her in the soothing voice he adopted for those of his clients he felt needed it. 'I'll get on to this Trimble fellow and insist on a copy.'

'Thank you, Robert,' Clare mumbled. She should have realized that was exactly what he would do. 'But I really don't think it is worth bothering about.'

'Of course it is. Now, I think we should begin to make some plans for us.'

'Yes, yes of course.' Clare tried to infuse some enthusiasm in to her voice. Whatever was the matter with her, for the last eighteen months at least she had longed for him to talk like this, even when she told herself that she liked things the way they were, that it was great to be independent. Now she felt almost as if she was suffocating in some nightmare situation of her own making. Twice she had thought she had broken free yet here she was again, being wined and dined and chatted up. She looked at him across the table; his face was almost as familiar as her own. For years he had been all she wanted, or thought she wanted, in life. Now suddenly she was questioning everything. She had even used the words 'breaking free' to herself. Hardly the language of love.

'Sorry, Robert, what did you say?' She realized he was looking at her, apparently waiting for an answer — to what?

His tone was level and patient, making Clare feel guilty again. 'I said I thought it would be a good idea if we both went back up there — next weekend, perhaps — and tried to sort things out.'

'No, no, I don't think that would be a good idea at all. I've told you — I don't think it is worth bothering about. The terms of the will are quite clear, and anyway it isn't enough to bother with — if I start contesting it there will be nothing left. I'd probably be out of pocket instead of getting anything.' She could hear her voice rising, and knew she was beginning to sound almost hysterical, so with a deep breath she forced herself to smile, then said calmly, 'It just isn't worth the trouble, Robert. I'm sorry I mentioned it — let's drop the subject.'

'If you say so. All the same . . . ' The last three words were almost inaudible, then with a dismissive shrug he added, 'We'll say no more.'

Clare did her best to give him her

undivided attention for the remainder of the evening, reminding herself that this was Robert, who had been her lover for two years, that they were to be married at last. But what had happened to the sparkle in their relationship? Surely it had been there once, hadn't it?

Robert was attentive and charming, and if he noticed anything lacking in her he didn't remark on it. He took her home and waited patiently on the doorstep while she fumbled for her key. Did he notice that she was also fumbling in her mind for a reasonable excuse not to let him in? She still hadn't found one when the door opened so she had little choice but to let him in.

She dropped her light stole over a chair and yawned exaggeratedly. Robert took her in his arms. 'Not that tired, surely, sweetheart?' he murmured as he bent to kiss her. Whatever answer she might have given was lost. The feel of him, the scent of him, everything about him was familiar and Clare found herself responding, in spite of herself. She decided she must have been suffering from some vague malaise of the feelings, perhaps.

'What would you like? Tea, coffee or a nightcap?' she murmured as they came up for air.

'The only nightcap I want is you,' he

whispered hoarsely against her hair.

Clare put her hands on his chest and pushed herself back from him so that she could look into his face. 'Robert, tell me, how come you have asked me to marry you all of a sudden?'

'All of a sudden!' He repeated her words with an accompanying guffaw of laughter. 'Hardly, my sweet, unless you call two years sudden.'

'You know what I mean. You've always said you couldn't marry me — there's always been a good reason. How come suddenly there isn't any more?'

'Come to bed . . . ' He took her hand and led her to the bedroom. Clare found herself hanging back.

'Don't fob me off, Robert, tell me.'

'But I did tell you — Linda has decided she does want a divorce, after all, and Annabel's old enough now to understand. So . . . ' He picked her up and placed her on the bed, puffing slightly from the exertion.

Clare accepted his explanation, just as she had done when he had been saying the opposite, and let him begin to remove her clothes. Feeling that more was expected of her than acquiescence, she started to unbutton his shirt. Impatiently, almost roughly, Robert pushed her hand aside and tore off his tie before finishing the job she had begun in such a desultory fashion and tossing his shirt after it. With something halfway between a moan and a grunt, he undid the waist of his trousers and unzipped his fly.

Feeling his hardness, Clare's earlier stirring died an abrupt death instead of becoming a full-blown arousal to match his. Robert didn't seem to notice that her quick intake of breath was one of pain not passion. When he finally dropped, with a satisfied sigh, on the pillow beside her, Clare felt cheated and angry. His performance, she felt, had been nearer rape than love-making. She remembered Zoe, in one of her more cynical moods, remarking that the way to a successful long-term relationship was the ability to fake it when you couldn't make it. Robert hadn't even given her the chance to do that.

She closed her eyes and pretended to be dropping into a satisfied doze when he murmured drowsily vague endearments. When his breathing relapsed into gentle snoring she cautiously removed the arm, now growing heavy, that was flung across her body, waited a few more minutes to be sure that she had not disturbed his sleep then very cautiously tiptoed to the bathroom. She closed the door behind her then turned the shower on, a long way from its full power so that it would not wake him, and stepped gratefully under the softly falling warm water. She felt — what? Defiled was too strong and biblically dramatic, but she did feel used and filled with a strong urge to wash and be clean again.

Robert was still asleep when she slid back between the sheets very carefully. After twenty minutes of lying stiff and straight on her back while her thoughts spiralled incessantly, she slid carefully off the bed again and switched on the electric jug in the tiny kitchen recess. With a hot mug of coffee cradled in her hands, she sat down in the lounge to think through this crazy situation she seemed to have landed herself in.

There was, she thought, some merit in Robert's idea of returning to Maldon to 'sort things out' but if she went it would be alone. The problem was how to achieve this. She half smiled to herself as she realized that she had thought of returning to Maldon, but it was nearby Castlemaine that Robert had spoken of. The difference being, of course, that while he was thinking of bearding Timothy Trimble in his office and going through that wretched will with him, she was thinking of Mark Fisk and his outrageous suggestion.

By the time Clare had drained her coffee she had worked out a plan of action. She rinsed out her coffee mug and tiptoed back to bed.

8

'Good heavens, is it that time already?' Clare's astonishment was quite genuine because she had dozed off again, quite unintentionally, to wake with a real start when Robert flung back the clothes and leapt off the bed.

'Eight thirty-five!' He glared at her as if she had personally made it that time. 'Don't you have an alarm clock?'

'I didn't set it,' Clare murmured drowsily, making no effort to get up herself.

'Why ever not?' Robert demanded, collecting his clothes together and heading for the shower.

'I didn't need to. I don't have to go into the office today — I have a free day.'

'Well I don't,' Robert shouted over the noise of the shower. 'I have a very full schedule and I'm going to be late.'

'Sorry,' Clare called back, thinking even as she did so that he probably wouldn't hear her.

Because she felt guilty she sat up, swung her legs over the side of the bed and then padded across to her robe before going back to the kitchen area and switching on the electric jug for a fresh pot of coffee.

'Toast?' she called when she heard the water stop and guessed he had stepped out of the shower.

'No thanks, I don't have time. Nor for coffee.' He sounded, Clare thought, thoroughly put out. 'I need to go home. I have to shave — can't go in looking like this.'

*   *   *

She waited till she heard his car leaving the kerb, then with a quick glance at the clock threw off her nightclothes and had one of the quickest showers of her life. By the time she came out, still towelling her hair, it was a few minutes after nine and she knew Zoe would be at the office.

'I can't come in today,' she told her. 'I . . . I'm sick.'

'You don't sound it — but I'll cover for you.'

Clare wondered, not for the first time, if it was a good idea having such a close friend as personal secretary. Zoe knew far too much about her, even how she sounded on the phone when she really was sick. But she couldn't worry about that now; she had bought time for herself, one whole day on her own, and she intended to make the most of it.

Munching an apple — she hadn't time for a formal breakfast — she flicked on the answering service, snatched up bag, car keys and phone, and less than a quarter of an hour behind Robert she left the flat.

She was humming to herself as she headed northward out of the city; she felt as if she had shed twenty years and was once more a schoolgirl playing truant. It was a heady feeling. By the time she was clear of the early morning snarl and was heading up the highway, however, rather different thoughts were kicking in. She wasn't entirely sure why she was doing this, certainly not what she intended to do on arrival, and was even less sure of her reception. What she did know was that there was something here that needed clearing up before she settled down to life with Robert.

'Life with Robert.' She found she was thinking of it in italics, or headlines, or stuck between inverted commas. It was something apart from her life to date. She should, she knew, be feeling on top of the world: wasn't this just what she had wanted for so long?

She drove straight to Maldon and drew up outside the flower shop. She found her heart was hammering with some suppressed excitement — or was it nervous apprehension? She locked her car deliberately, adopting a cool and nonchalant attitude, and strolled across the few feet of pavement to the door of the shop. She felt strangely breathless as she wrapped her fingers round the door knob. Nothing happened; it refused to turn. It was locked. A quick glance at her watch told her that it was nearer eleven o'clock than ten. Why was it closed? She looked round her as if the answer would be in her surroundings and only then saw the small notice on the door. Written on the blank side of a business card in rather pale biro it was far from obvious. *Closed till further notice*, she read.

The anti-climax surged through her in the form of unreasonable irritation. She rattled the knob; maybe Mark was in there somewhere. Well, there was no way now she could stroll casually in and make out she just happened to be passing. If she wanted to see Mark she would have to seek him out — very deliberately — and go to the cottage. She turned away reluctantly and got back in her car.

She drove the short distance to the cottage, mulling over in her mind just what she was going to say, how she was going to explain her presence without looking as if she had run up here specifically to see Mark. A big ask considering that was exactly what she was doing.

Clare didn't know whether to be pleased or not to see Mark's car parked outside the cottage. She was sitting in her own car, taking a deep breath before she went to the door, eyes closed, when a sharp tap on her window made her sit up with a start. Her lids flew open and she found herself staring through the glass into the vivid blue eyes of Mark Fisk. He tapped the glass again and she switched the ignition back on and pressed the appropriate button to lower the window.

'You made me jump,' she complained.

'What are you doing here?'

Mark grinned at her accusation as if he found it very amusing. 'What are you doing here?' he asked again.

'Me? Oh, I was just passing,' Clare tossed off airily.

'Yeah, sure. Just passing. Where from and where to?'

'Does it matter?' Clare intended to sound distant — lofty — but was afraid her voice only came out as a petulant whine. 'What were you doing, anyway, knocking on my window like that, startling me?'

'Heard a car, came out to see if it was anyone I know and, lo and behold, it was you. Turned up again like a bad penny.' Clare wasn't at all sure she cared for that remark. 'Well, are you going to sit there all day registering, for some reason, righteous indignation or are you coming in for a cup of coffee?'

'You haven't asked me.'

'Yes I have — I just did. Are you coming?' As he spoke Mark snatched her door open so suddenly that Clare almost fell out at his feet.

'Oh all right,' she said ungraciously, as she stepped out of the car. 'But weren't you going somewhere? Don't let me stop you.'

'I told you I just came out to see who was parking outside my gate.' He put his hand under her elbow, leaving her barely time to lock her car before she found herself being propelled towards the house.

'Why is the shop closed?' she wanted to know.

'I'll answer that when you give me a satisfactory explanation for your sudden appearance on my doorstep.'

'I wasn't on your doorstep,' she protested feebly, realizing that now she was, and wondering why her elbow was tingling so.

By the time they reached the kitchen, Mark still with his hand on her elbow as if she might dematerialize or something at any moment, Clare was beginning to feel rather as she imagined Alice must have felt when she went down the rabbit hole. Not quite sure where she was or even who she was.

When Mark let her go to make coffee, she dropped down on the nearest kitchen chair as if without his support she could no longer stand. For some reason she could not take her eyes off him; after all, making coffee was not such a fascinating pastime. She had forgotten how pleasing he was to the eye, how graceful in his movements. She dropped her eyes, feeling embarrassed when he turned towards her and handed her a large mug of steaming coffee. He pulled up a kitchen stool and dropped down on the other side of the table. He looked down at her with a quizzical grin. Clare, sitting on a chair, not a stool, was forced to look up at him, or not look at him at all.

She chose the latter option, lowered her eyes and concentrated on sipping the hot coffee.

'Have you come to give me an answer?' She looked up, startled, when he broke the silence. What did he mean? Mark looked back at her, waiting for her reply.

'To what?' she finally croaked.

'To my question, of course. Or offer — whichever way you care to look at it.'

Clare stared back at him, annoyed to feel the warm colour rising up her neck and throat and flooding her cheeks, remembering that the last time she had seen him he had asked her to marry him.

'Oh, that . . . ' Her voice was studiedly cool, but she could not prevent the faint quaver it seemed to have developed. 'But I knew you didn't mean that — it was just a joke.'

He stared back at her, and the brilliant blue of his eyes struck her again and she was once more aware of their hypnotic power. Finally he shook his head slowly. 'No. No joke, Clare. I meant it. The offer was genuine. So, have you thought about it?'

'Of course not.' She forced herself to look away and concentrate on her coffee. 'I thought it was a joke — and not a very good one.'

'Are you saying no?'

She got up and walked across to the sink, where she carefully placed her empty coffee mug on the draining board. She remained there, looking out of the window with her back to the room — and Mark.

'Of course I am. I couldn't marry you anyway — even if I wanted to,' she explained to the well of silence that filled the kitchen. 'I'm going to marry someone else.' She heard the stool scrape back and when a second later it fell on the floor she was startled into spinning round to find herself facing Mark. She was looking directly at him. Moreover, he had grabbed her by both arms just above the elbow and she couldn't escape, even if she had any willpower left. The sense of unreality had taken over completely and she found herself moving closer, instead of breaking free, and melting into his embrace.

As if from a place just outside her own body, she saw herself turn her face up and watched her lips part to meet his.

'You shouldn't be kissing me like that,' Mark told her when they finally drew apart.

'I thought you were kissing me,' Clare protested. 'What do you mean, anyway? Didn't you enjoy it?'

'As much as you did,' he answered ambiguously. 'But all the same, you shouldn't be kissing me like that when you are going to marry someone else.'

'Oh. No, you're probably right,' Clare agreed, but made no effort to move out of his arms, and he made not the slightest effort to release her.

Only when he asked in a voice that sounded slightly peeved, 'Then why are you?' did she raise her head and, leaning back in his arms, look up into his face.

'Are you asking me why I kissed you — or why I am marrying someone else?'

'Both.'

Clare frowned slightly. 'I guess because I said I would.'

'I didn't hear you say you would kiss me, you just did it, so I suppose you are talking about getting married Do you really want to?'

She shook her head. 'Not at this moment.'

'Clare Davenport, you are an odd person. I would never have said you were the sort of person to do things just because someone said you should. You weren't like that with me, anyway, yet . . . ' Mark dropped his hands abruptly to his sides so that without their support Clare almost lost her balance. 'I think we need to talk,' he told her. 'I'll make more coffee.' He turned to the stove and Clare dropped back into her chair. He put their two mugs on a small tray. 'We'll take it outside.'

When they were sitting opposite each other at the garden table he said, 'Now tell me.'

'Tell you what?' Clare prevaricated. Removed slightly from his physical presence, she felt more in command of herself and rather, at this moment, as if she was being interviewed for a job or hauled up before the principal at school.

'Don't hedge, Clare. I want to know why you won't marry me, but you are happy to spend the rest of your life with that stuffed shirt.'

'I said I would. We've been an item for two years. He's not really so . . . stuffy.'

'Which, of course, is why you responded as you did when I kissed you.'

'That was — different,' she muttered, knowing that was not an answer. Her eyes were lowered but she looked up when he banged his mug down on the metal table, and was startled to see the mocking, almost bantering look had left his face and been replaced by anger.

'Grow up and stop playing games.' She flinched at the tone of his voice.

'I don't know what you mean.'

'Of course you do. I asked you to marry me. I meant it. Oh, I admit the idea first occurred to me as a good way out of the ridiculous impasse old Hester has made with this will of hers, then I realized that I did mean it, I would like to marry you. Now you coolly tell me you can't because you are going to marry someone else and at the same time kiss me like . . . well . . . You know how you kissed me. At least you could explain, couldn't you?'

Clare stared at him, searching for the right words, but before she found them he spoke again. 'When you were up here I didn't think you had any attachments. I was a tad concerned that Timothy might charm you. I heard that some guy came chasing up here after you and you sent him off with his tail between his legs, so naturally I thought the field was clear.'

Clare twisted her coffee mug in her hands. 'Yes,' she murmured, 'Robert did come up here after me, and yes — I did. Well, it wasn't very pleasant and I was annoyed because I thought I had finished it before I left Melbourne. Now, well . . . it's so difficult.'

'Is it? I am probably being very obtuse but what's happened that has made you change your mind about him? If you weren't pleased to see him when he came up here after you then why in the name of all that's holy are you considering marrying him?'

'I feel . . . obliged to.' Clare's voice dropped to a whisper as if she was admitting to something that she felt really ashamed about.

'Obliged to? Why? Are you pregnant?'

'No, no, of course not. It's just that . . . well, I've known him for two years and for most of that time there has been an understanding between us that we would marry . . . one day. Now his wife is divorcing him so . . . well, I feel obliged to marry him.'

'What absolute crap!' Mark exploded. 'There is only one reason to marry anyone — because you want to, really want to, because . . . ' He finished the sentence almost

176

inaudibly to himself. 'You don't feel you can live without them.' He looked up and smiled suddenly. 'Well, Clare Davenport, I guess I've lived without you long enough to go on doing it if I have to, but I have to admit I enjoyed having you around in the shop and I enjoy your company. I thought you had spunk — now I'm not so sure.'

'I loved it!' she admitted. 'Being in the shop, I mean. I reckon we could . . . ' She trailed off before she said too much, but it was true: it had been hard work at times but she had relished every moment working in the little shop and had enjoyed thinking of ways to make it a paying proposition.

'Do you enjoy your work, your career, in Melbourne in the same way?'

Slowly Clare shook her head. 'That's different. That is my living. The week I spent in Flowers For The Journey was . . . it was almost like a holiday.'

'Then why did you run away back to Melbourne?'

'I have to make a living.'

'There is a big difference in making a living and living; one is just working to exist, the other doing what you enjoy.'

'Oh, spare me the sermon,' Clare snapped. 'I make a good living — I earn enough to do the things I enjoy.'

'But you don't particularly enjoy your work.'

'Sometimes, but I do feel at times a bit depressed by it. After all, as a divorce lawyer all I do is untangle people from the relationships they have entered into. It makes one a bit cynical.'

'And now you are considering making a marriage yourself that has Buckley's hope of being a success.'

Clare shot to her feet. 'What I do and do not do is entirely my business and nothing whatever to do with you, Mark Fisk.' She glared at him. 'I think I should go — this conversation is pointless.'

'Go then — take the easy way. I agree it is pointless discussing anything with someone as stupid, stubborn and blind as you. Go on — be successful — but don't expect to be happy!'

'I will!' She glared defiantly across the garden table at him, and he stood up and glared back. Then it hit her; if she flounced out in a temper again, if she went back to Robert, safe, dependable, dull Robert, and her rut of a career, she would never see Mark again, never know what happened to the shop, this house, even Boris. The prospect was suddenly so bleak she burst into tears.

How she got there she didn't know, but she

was in his arms again. He was holding her close. Pushing her hair back from her wet face as if she were a small child. 'I'm sorry . . . ' he was murmuring. 'I didn't mean to upset you. I just felt so mad, so furious, to see you stepping into a future without any highs and lows. That's not the way to live. You probably thought you loved this guy because no one had taught you different, but why on earth did you land yourself in a job that it's quite obvious you don't either enjoy or even think really worthwhile?'

'It's what I'm qualified for,' she protested. 'Anyway, how do you know that's the way I feel about my job? I never said so. I don't even know that I do. If I don't know, what makes you think you do?'

'Simple deduction. If you really thought your high-powered job was as emotionally satisfying as you would like it to be, you wouldn't be chucking your life away on a man you don't really love, who has just become a habit, simply because you feel your biological clock is running out. You actually enjoyed working in the flower shop.'

Clare gaped at him, wondering how he managed to know so much about her. 'What are you, some sort of shrink?' she demanded. Then, sounding more surprised than angry, 'You are right, I did enjoy the flower shop. I found I wanted it to succeed. I can't think why — considering everything. I thought maybe . . . I even got to like, or at least not mind too much, working with you . . . ' She trailed off, feeling she had said either too much, or too little, she wasn't sure. 'Well, are you?' she demanded. Clarifying when he looked blank, she said, 'Are you a psychologist or something?'

'No, far from it. I'm an accountant.'

'Oh. Well . . . ' They stood and stared at one another, then Mark held out his hand towards her. 'Now we seem to have cleared the air a bit, let's go back inside and get things really straight. Then you can go back to Melbourne and pick up the threads there if that is what you are sure you want. If not . . . ' He left the other option vaguely in the air and, taking her hand, led her back into the house.

Indoors she excused herself and went to the bathroom to repair the damage to her face. When she returned she found Mark sitting at the table, which was spread with papers. He looked serious and businesslike.

'I'm not going to ask you to marry me again,' he told her, 'but I do want you to think very seriously about what you really want to do. If you are absolutely certain that you want to continue your life as it was before this bombshell of Hester's making disrupted things for you, then that's it. No more discussion. If, however, there is the faintest feeling that you may not be doing the right thing after all — that you would really like to take up your inheritance, start a completely new way of life — then I'll go through these papers and accounts very thoroughly with you. It's your decision entirely.'

Clare looked at him; she had felt an odd pang when he said he wasn't going to ask her to marry him again. Then she remembered what he had said about the difference between making a living and living. 'I want to live,' she told him. 'But before you begin on those accounts — or whatever they are — I'd like to ask a few questions myself.' Clare could hear she was using her 'talking to clients voice'. She thought of it in her head, as her 'sympathetic lawyer' voice. She cleared her throat and added, in a more everyday voice, 'If you don't mind.'

'Fire away!' Mark said cheerfully.

'Well, first, why aren't you at the shop today?'

'Because I am here, with you. Second?'

'Well, what are you really doing messing about in that shop at all?'

'Anything else?'

'No. well, yes . . . ' Clare hesitated, not

quite sure how to phrase her next question. Mark waited patiently. She took a deep breath. 'Well, I couldn't help wondering . . . well, what I mean is, why are you living in Hester's house?' The words finally came in a rush and try as she might, somehow they managed to sound suspicious and accusatory.

Mark laughed. 'I think I'll start at the end and work back to the beginning. The reason I am in the house is very simple — because of that canine monster out there. If he had to go into kennels for any length of time his board and keep would very much reduce the cash available for whoever finally inherits.' The tone of his voice didn't quite match his words and Clare realized with some surprise that he was actually attached to the animal. 'As to why I am messing about in that shop — your words not mine — I guess the answer to that one is I am a woolly-headed idealist. I wanted to get out of an office, away from figures, and do something else with my life. I like flowers and I like people. Put the two together and you have a florist's shop. Bingo! I thought, that is what I will do with the rest of my life. Unfortunately I found that to make any sort of a go of it I had to be in an office, juggling — or trying to juggle — figures. I'm not at the shop today because, quite simply, I lost heart — or came to my senses. I realized when I woke up this morning that there was no way I was going to get Flowers For The Journey on its feet. Not without an injection of capital and someone to help me. So I stayed home to stew in my own juice and work out what to do next.'

'And have you?'

'Worked out what to do next, you mean? Nope — I've stewed plenty but I am no nearer an answer.' Mark rubbed his chin in a rueful gesture. 'I was an accountant — well, still am, I suppose, so I thought getting the figures straight for a little business like that would be a breeze.'

'Who ran it before?'

'Old Hester herself — quite successfully for a while — but then she seemed to lose interest and when she was taken sick and she was hardly there any business there was fell right away. When I delved into the books it seemed that she hadn't actually been making any money for a long time; quite the reverse, she was actually losing it. Finding that out was the last straw — I chucked it in. Thing was I was just beginning to enjoy the challenge the week you were in the shop, thought together we might be able to make a go of it. Now how about that for cock-eyed optimism?'

Clare's lips curved in a small half-smile.

'Full marks!' she told him. 'But I have to admit that I was beginning to enjoy it too.'

'Then why did you run off back to the big smoke? Do you really prefer undoing other people's marriages to building up a worthwhile business?'

Clare bridled. 'I don't do the breaking of marriages, you know. My clients have already done that for themselves. I just help them sort out the mess and make some sort of sense out of the situation. And yes, I did enjoy my work at first. But now — I don't quite know why — it seems to have lost some of its savour somehow.' Clare shrugged. 'I guess I have probably just got stale — need a good holiday . . . '

'Or a total change of lifestyle,' Mark suggested. Clare ignored this.

'But why on earth did Hester make such a crazy will? Robert says Timothy Trimble should never have let her. He certainly wouldn't! Robert is a lawyer too.' Clare tagged on the last words as explanation for quoting Robert and mentioning him at all.

'He probably thinks that, but he didn't know your Great Aunt Hester. I somehow think she might have been more than a match for him too!'

'You obviously did know her — very well,' Clare remarked drily, adding, when curiosity got the better of her, 'Tell me about her. How did you get so involved?'

'I thought I told you — I was brought up in this house.'

'You told me your mother worked for my aunt.'

'Well, yes, so she did — I suppose you would call it that. But it wasn't your usual mistress/servant relationship — '

'Goodness, what an old-fashioned expression!' Clare interrupted. 'But if it wasn't that, what was it?'

'My mother was Hester McMaster's dresser when — '

'Dresser! You mean she was on the stage?'

'If you're going to keep interrupting me I shall never finish — but, yes, she was on the stage. That's if you call music hall the stage? She wasn't a famous Shakespearean actress or anything like that but she was fairly well known in her day.'

'Go on. I'll try not to interrupt any more,' Clare promised. Mentally she was rapidly trying to change her picture of Hester McMaster, but she had formed such a strong image of a faded gentlewoman in her mind that it was difficult to discard it and replace it with the more colourful one that Mark's words suggested. 'I suppose,' she added, more or less to herself, 'that is where the money came from.'

185

'Well, it doesn't take a genius, does it, to know it didn't come from Flowers For The Journey!' Mark snapped, adding waspishly, 'That's where a lot of it went, though — there and to my father.'

9

'You told me you had no father,' Clare accused, remembering what Mark had told her before about his childhood.

'I didn't — thanks be to God — because Hester McMaster paid him a regular sum to stay away from my mother and me. He went to England and I believe he died there when I was still young.'

'You mean he was a remittance man? Paid to keep away?'

'Yes — only it was usually the other way around, English aristocracy paying people to stay out here in the far-flung colonies. My father was paid to stay in England.'

'But why?'

'Why? Because he was every sort of a son of a bitch. He seduced my mother.' Clare suppressed a smile at his use of what she thought of as another old-fashioned expression; she guessed he must have learned these from his elderly benefactress. 'Then he left her and when he came back knocked her about.'

'Were your parents married?' Clare enquired with some hesitation.

'Oh yes, old Hester saw to that. She was a stickler for things being done right — unfortunately. She didn't want me to grow up under the shadow of illegitimacy.'

'But . . . ' Clare was about to say it wasn't such a disability these days when he continued, guessing at her thoughts.

'You have to remember what the climate was when she was young. She thought it would be the ruin of both my mother and myself. As it turned out, marriage nearly was. From the little I learned from my mother, he made life such hell for both of us, for all of us, that eventually Hester paid him to keep away.'

'And your mother?'

'My mother is dead.'

'I . . . see,' Clare murmured, endeavouring to sound sympathetic while wondering how long ago she had died.

'She's been dead for twenty years,' Mark supplied, as if she had actually asked the question. His expression hardened as he added with considerable bitterness, 'I was seventeen at the time and had taken myself off to England with some crazy quixotic notion of finding my father and . . . Well, I don't quite know what I would have done if I had found him. Hester got in touch with me to tell me my mother was sick — but it was too late, she was dead before I could get to

188

her. But I came back anyway.'

'That was good of you,' Clare murmured.

'You think so? Callous and calculating, more like — I knew I was about all the old girl had left. I also knew that she cared for me — almost thought of me as a son. She supported me until I was qualified and able to do it for myself.'

'Oh, what did you qualify as?' Before she had finished asking, Clare remembered that he had told her he was an accountant. The look he threw her said he remembered too. She could see he was irritated, and also by her interruption.

They remained silent for a space, Clare careful not to arrest his narrative again, but Mark seemed temporarily lost in some hinterworld of his own, his eyes gazing into space while his mind ran backwards. 'Which explains why I'm bothering about you,' he said at last, turning his attention back to her.

'It does?'

'It does,' he repeated. 'I feel I have had more than my share from the late Hester McMaster and if she wanted to ferret out an unknown niece, who is at least a blood relation, then I owe it to her to make sure, as best I can, that her wishes are carried out.'

'But if I don't inherit, then who does? Do you?'

'I must say you are pretty slow on the uptake for a lady of the law.' His sudden grin took any sting from his words. 'I should have thought you could have worked that out for yourself if our esteemed Mr Trimble didn't enlighten you.'

'The question of who got what if I didn't never came up,' Clare answered stiffly. 'The thought however did cross my mind that the longer things went on and the more difficulty there was about settling this inheritance, the more T.T. would gain from the whole business.'

Mark's smiled widened. 'I like that — the abbreviation, I mean. Suits him to a T!'

'You don't like him?'

Mark shrugged. 'Not always, but I'm quite fond of him. In fact, you could say he is my closest friend. When we were children I used to accuse him of being a smarmy little prick; sucking up to old Hester. That was not really fair of me. He was just naturally virtuous and law-abiding and I was not. I've known him for ever — we are the same age. He lived next door as a child, we played together before we started school and of course went to the same schools.'

'I see,' Clare said, wondering if she really did. He still hadn't explained about this confusing inheritance. 'You still haven't explained just what happens if I refuse to accept the terms and walk away from the whole thing,' she complained.

'What do you want explaining?'

'Well, why the shop seems to be such a white elephant. I should have thought it would have been a little goldmine in a tourist place like Maldon. Couldn't Hester have got someone else in to run it when she couldn't? You, for instance?'

Clare watched his face harden and his lips lose their smiling fullness and become a hard line. 'I'll tell you why — it's very simple, really. Old Hester was a stubborn old bat — she would go on trying to run the thing and make it pay when she was well past it. But I was much worse — I was both stubborn and selfish. I should have made allowances, bitten my tongue, not argued with her over the damn place. Certainly not rowed with her about it.' He gave a small bitter laugh that was totally without humour. 'Well, she had the last word when she died!' There was a long pause while Clare thrashed around in her mind for something to say but found nothing. 'So now here I am trying to expunge my guilt by helping you get what is yours.'

'I see,' Clare murmured once more, but his explanation, such as it was, had left her more confused than before.

Mark went on, looking not at her but at a spot somewhere behind her and over her shoulder; he seemed to be talking to someone else, or himself, more than to her. 'I am an accountant by trade, or profession, if you prefer. I could see, or thought I could see, what needed to be done to make Flowers For The Journey pay handsomely. I pointed out to Hester what needed to be done, but she had her own way of doing things, her own thoughts about the shop, and she refused to listen, much less implement any of my suggestions. Finally we came to a real humdinger of a verbal battle over it and I flew back to Western Australia, back to being an accountant. I was lucky: the firm I had been in before took me back because my replacement had just left. Six months later she was dead. I should have realized how sick she was. I flew straight back, for her funeral, to find the shop just about moribund. I should have come sooner, swallowed my pride, but the least I could do when I did get here was look after poor old Boris, and try and hold things together till you took over. It didn't occur to me you would refuse.'

'The terms being what they are I have little alternative,' Clare responded stiffly, her cool tones in no way reflecting the turbulence of her inner emotions. Quite suddenly she found herself empathizing with this unknown relative. She didn't particularly want to feel like that — it was a weakness she felt that could lead to, well, anything. In a deliberately cool voice she asked, 'Why did she call the shop Flowers For The Journey?'

Mark smiled reminiscently. 'It was not a very original name. She came across a bookshop called Books For The Journey — the name and the idea it represented appealed to her. She said to me, 'If books, why not flowers?' After all, people often give flowers to someone who is leaving on a journey of some sort, hence airport flower shops which, as far as I can see, do pretty well. I pointed out that people also buy flowers to greet those who are arriving. She brushed that aside and called her shop Flowers For The Journey.'

Clare thought this a nice idea. She thought of wedding flowers, and even funeral wreaths, both marking the start of a journey of sorts. 'I rather wish I had known old Hester personally,' she murmured thoughtfully then, recalling why she was really here, mentally and metaphorically tightened up her thoughts and said, somewhat tartly, 'Thank you for your explanations, Mark. But you still haven't told me just why you seemed to think it would be the solution to everything if you and I got married. I can see a host of problems arising from such an action — but not one solution.'

He looked at Clare as if he found it very hard indeed to believe anyone could be so dumb. He sighed and then in that 'trying so hard to be patient' voice of someone explaining something very simple to a person of very limited intelligence said, slowly and carefully, 'No one — certainly not Hester and not even T.T. — could have any valid objection to you leaving the shop, house and dog in charge of your husband during the week and returning here for the weekends. You could continue your soliciting life in Melbourne while I ran the shop. With your legal expertise and my accounting knowledge it would be a pity if we couldn't make it a success.'

At this point, Clare, who had been staring at him, not quite open-mouthed, exploded, amazing not only Mark but herself with the intensity of the white-hot spiral of anger rising inside her.

'What you are suggesting is that I marry you in order to inherit that bloody little shop and this lovely house so that you can reap the benefits! Of all the crackpot dodgy ideas, that beats them all! Good God, it's downright immoral — and a very poor deal for me!'

'Hold on!' Mark held up a hand to silence her. 'Poor deal? What's so bad about it? You get a business, a partner to run it for you, a house that, on your own admission you love, and possibly some cash as this way you won't be wasting any assets on going to law and lining the pockets of people like our friend Timothy. What's more' — he paused and grinned at her — 'you get a husband into the bargain!'

'For starters, I don't need a husband, I have one lined up. Secondly, I don't want to live in Maldon and commute to Melbourne. Thirdly, I don't want that bloody dog and — and — even — if I did want a husband it wouldn't be you!' She ended on a rising note as she got to her feet and snatched up her bag, and flung at him as her parting shot, 'The whole idea is so absolutely ridiculous that I am not staying here another minute to discuss it or even think about it . . . ' At this point she ran out of steam and registered the fact that Mark was merely looking at her with an amused expression on his face which served to infuriate her further. To cap it all, she couldn't lay her hand on her car keys.

'Methinks the lady does protest too much . . . '

'Don't quote Shakespeare at me either!' Clare raged, fumbling wildly in her bag for her keys. She found them, and in her agitation somehow managed to flip them on to the floor, where Mark immediately snatched them up.

'Give me those!' Clare demanded.

He smiled, and clenched his fingers tighter over them.

'Give me them!' Clare screeched, feeling that she was rapidly losing the plot and enraged with herself for doing so. Desperately she lunged towards him and tried to snatch them from him, only to find her wrist caught in the iron grip of his other hand. 'Oh!' Her breath caught on a sob of rage and frustration and she managed to kick him on the shins so that he too gave a yelp of pain before he pulled her close to him. With another 'Oh . . . ' on quite a different note, she found herself unable to fight any more as her treacherous body melded into his and his lips on hers cut off any further protest.

When he finally released her she sank back on to her chair, mainly because her legs didn't seem keen on the idea of supporting her. Mark sat down again opposite her. She watched him drop her keys into the pocket of his jeans and held out her hand. 'May I have them?' With a supreme effort she kept her voice level.

'But of course — I have no wish to have an unwilling hostage. But before I hand them over, will you grant me one favour?'

'What?'

'Half an hour at least of your time to talk this suggestion of mine through. I'll let you go first — tell me calmly, and logically, without emotion, why you think it is so outlandish?'

Clare, still shaken by the way she had responded to Mark, took another deep breath and endeavoured to be as he suggested, calm and logical, the sort of person she was when she dealt with the unravelling of other folk's matrimonial messes.

'Well, it's . . . it's crazy to tie ourselves up to each other in a legal bond like marriage just to get hold of property.' Mark sat silent, listening, so she was forced to continue. 'We don't love each other — we don't even know each other very well. I have a home and work in Melbourne and . . . I am supposed to be marrying someone else.' She stopped, feeling she had argued her case very feebly. She shrugged rather helplessly. 'Well, that's it. I can't say any more.'

Into the ensuing silence Mark finally asked, 'This person you are marrying — tell me about him, please?'

'What do you want to know? And anyway I don't see that it is relevant at all. I am going to marry someone else so that precludes any possibility that I could marry you.'

'Tell me about him,' Mark repeated. 'What sort of a person is he? How long have you known him? Most important, why are you marrying him? Is it just because you feel your biological clock is ticking away rather inexorably?'

'No! No, it is not!' Clare retorted indignantly, yet even as she said the words she was uncomfortably aware that the thought was there — in the back of her mind, but there. 'I'm marrying Robert because . . .' To her annoyance her voice petered out as she tried to bring to the forefront of her mind the reasons she had given herself so many times for marrying Robert. 'Well, he asked me.' How feeble that sounded; she must do better than that. 'I've known him, very well, for more than two years — '

'If it's taken you so long to decide to marry him then I don't think you should,' Mark interrupted.

'Oh, but it hasn't!' Clare protested. 'There was a . . . problem.'

'A wife?' Mark interjected again.

'Yes but — oh, stop interrupting me, will you, please!'

'And now there is no wife?' he continued just as if she had said nothing.

'No. Well, yes — that is, I'm not sure. I

think she has left him or something. Anyway, he's asked me to marry him — and after wanting him to I can't suddenly turn round and refuse, can I, now . . . ' Clare's voice trailed away as she realized what she had been about to say. As she knew he would, Mark said it for her.

'Now that you realize you don't want to marry him after all.'

Clare felt colour rising up her throat to burn in her cheeks, but it was anger as much as embarrassment. She shot to her feet. 'This is ridiculous!' she stormed, holding out an imperious hand. 'Give me my keys back at once!'

Mark put his hand in the pocket of his jeans and she saw his fingers curl over her keys. But he did not bring them out and she knew he was just tightening his grip on them. 'You have totally failed to convince me,' he told her.

'I don't have to convince you of anything. Give me my keys!'

'I don't think you have convinced yourself either,' Mark went on just as if she had not spoken.

Clare sat down again; she was beginning to feel ridiculous standing over him demanding her keys back. She slumped in her chair with her chin on her chest but jerked her head up rapidly when he said in a voice that seemed to her cold and without feeling of any kind, 'I suppose you think it is about time that you legalized the situation?'

'Yes. No. I . . .'

'Come on, Clare, you surely don't expect me to believe there was nothing more than the occasional chaste kiss between you for two years? Someone as attractive as you?'

Absurdly she wanted to ask him if he really thought she was attractive but all she did was murmur, 'No, I am not expecting you to believe that at all. What I am hoping you will understand is why I can't back out now and say I am not going to marry him.'

'Can't say I do, but I can see that you don't really want to marry him any more than you do me — so at least he and I are on a level playing field.'

Clare stared at him, knowing with a terrible clarity that what he was saying was correct. 'God damn you!' she yelled, her voice breaking on a sob. 'You're right, I don't want to marry anyone — anyone! Now please just give me my keys and let me go.'

To her chagrin, Mark merely smiled and said with obvious amusement, 'Wow! You must be a sensation in court if you put on turns like that!'

Clare glared, took a deep, deep breath and

said calmly, 'I would like my keys, please.'

He continued to ignore her request. 'Look at it this way. Clare, I am giving you a wonderful escape route. You simply tell this Robert guy that you are sorry, but you have met this quite fabulous person — me — and that we are getting married therefore you can't marry him.'

'B-but . . . ' Clare stammered feebly.

'We can get married with as much speed as possible. You can collect your inheritance and in due course you can divorce me — that should be easy enough for you, as you are in the trade, so to speak — and there you are. Free of me, free of him, but with a very nice house. Everyone is happy — especially old Hester up there who after all only wanted you to have it.'

'Yes but — ' Clare tried again.

'I shan't make any demands or advances. It shall be — what is it they call it? — a marriage in name only.'

'Sounds very calculating and mercenary,' she murmured weakly. Feeling the first stirring of temptation, she did love the house.

'But of course, I am calculating and mercenary,' Mark acknowledged. 'I also owe an enormous debt to Hester and I really cared for her. I would like to think that we were doing something to enable her last wishes to be carried out.'

'Put like that . . . ' Clare murmured weakly.

'I knew you would come round to my way of thinking,' Mark said cheerfully. He put his hand in his pocket and, drawing out her keys, tossed them casually on to the table between them. 'Here you are — you can go now if you want to!'

Clare picked them up slowly, reluctantly; she was not sure, not sure at all that she did.

Her anger had abated as quickly as it had blown up. She didn't move but fumbled with her bunch of keys till she had the ignition key for her car between the thumb and forefinger of her right hand. 'Well, I suppose I should make tracks.' She tried to sound firm and decided but her voice came out the very opposite, wavering and totally unsure.

'I suppose you should.'

Clare turned away and took a few steps then turned back to him. Mark was watching her, unsmiling. Somehow she found that more unnerving than when he grinned unashamedly at her. She had got used to him looking like that.

'Look, I'm really not happy with this arrangement.'

'With the arrangement — or with me?'

'Both. It doesn't seem right — not really ethical, somehow.'

Mark made a sound that was somewhere between a 'tch' and a sigh; it expressed his impatience with her and his exasperation perfectly.

'If you are going to change your mind, do it now. Don't drive back to Melbourne chewing the whole thing over and ring me up when you get there to tell me you have ditched me.'

'Ditched you! God, Mark, this is supposed to be some sort of cold-blooded business arrangement — so there is no need to use emotive language like that.'

'Well then, why don't you stay here and make some cold-blooded arrangements for carrying out this deal?'

Clare sighed, returned to her seat and sat down. 'Maybe it would be better to get myself clear of, well, of Robert, before I start arranging that.'

'Ah yes — always better to be off with the old love before you are on with the new.'

'Who said anything about love?' Clare retorted somewhat acidly.

'No one. So let's get down to brass tacks. This is, after all, a business arrangement.'

'Yes,' Clare agreed, feeling curiously deflated.

'If we are going to do this, the sooner the better, so any suggestions as to where, when and how?'

'ASAP and with minimal fuss.'

'You mean no ceremony, no gorgeous gown, no bridesmaids, no good nosh afterwards?'

'That is exactly what I mean.'

'As you say.' Mark shrugged. 'Your place or mine? In other words, Melbourne or Maldon?'

'Melbourne, I think.' Clare felt this would have the dual advantage of being more convenient for her and possibly more anonymous.

'Fine — then as the expert, can I leave you to organize things?'

'I suppose so.' Clare sounded less than enthusiastic and in truth was already wondering what mad scheme she was getting into.

'I can't believe I'm doing this because of a dog,' she grumbled.

'You are doing it, my dear Clare, to get a house — and I am doing it to get a business. The dog is incidental.'

Clare thought that whatever Boris was, he was not, and never would be, incidental.

As she stood by her car, Clare looked back at the house, wondering if she was stark staring raving mad. It was so lovely, the house she had always dreamed of, sometimes quite literally; the afternoon sun warmed and mellowed the old stones so that it seemed to glow with a light of its own. She felt a curious reluctance to leave it. Telling herself she was not being sentimental and fanciful as well as a fool, she got in her car and switched on the ignition. At least, she thought, there was no question now of her marrying Robert — once she had surmounted the small hurdle of actually telling him that she was marrying someone else. She drove home in a dream and found a message from Robert on her answering service saying that he was taking her out to dinner that night.

How like him, she thought, to tell her — not ask her. Well, she had something to tell him too, and on that thought she picked up the phone to call him back. She got his answering service.

'I'm afraid I can't come out to dinner with you tonight — but call round for a drink,' she told him.

$$\star \quad \star \quad \star$$

Clare's heart sank when she opened the door to him; she could see that he was not pleased. 'What do you mean, you can't come out for dinner? I've booked the table,' he told her.

'I have something to say to you, Robert.

Please, sit down. What would you like to drink?'

He didn't answer, but walked over to her drinks tray and poured himself a whisky. Clare was surprised at the strength of her annoyance at the way he took it quite for granted that he was at home in her flat. Almost as an afterthought, he turned to her. 'Sherry, I suppose?'

'No, I'll have a whisky too.' Sherry would not adequately give her the courage to say what had to be said. She accepted the glass and took a gulp that was far too big and nearly robbed her of any speech. 'I'm not going to marry you.' It was out in a rush and she took a slightly more restrained sip.

Robert stared at her in a silence that lasted so long Clare wondered if he had heard. 'What do you mean?' he asked at last. 'Of course you are — it's been understood for ages that one day we would get married.'

'Has it? Well, I'm sorry, but it seems too late now.'

'Too late? What on earth do you mean? I have always said when Annabel is old enough to cope with her parents divorcing we would get married. Well, now she is. We had an understanding, you and I.'

Clare was barely listening to his protests.

'I'm marrying someone else.' The words came out in a rush.

'You can't be — you don't know anyone,' Robert protested, spluttering in his surprise and fury. 'Except that wretched little lawyer, the one up in Castlemaine — who was so insufferable when I came to see you.'

Clare laughed, a rather hysterical high-pitched laugh; she had forgotten all about Timothy Trimble and his altercation with Robert. 'No, not him — someone else. You haven't met him. We're getting married in a couple of weeks or so.'

'A couple of weeks!' Robert latched on to this and gulped his whisky, his face suffused with fury and, it seemed to Clare, actually darkening with rage. 'You can't . . . ' He paused briefly as another thought struck him. 'You must have known him — been carrying on with him for ages while — I can't believe it of you, Clare. How could you?'

Clare was about to deny this accusation, then saw it as a way out. 'Well, you had better believe it. You have strung me along using Annabel as an excuse. Yes, excuse — you didn't want to turn your cosy life upside down, but now Linda has done it for you. She's beaten you to it, left you before you could leave her, hasn't she?' She held out a hand when it looked as if he intended to interrupt her. 'I am not really blaming you — I was just as much to blame, letting you do that to me.'

'I was always straight with you. I never said I would marry you until Annabel was launched.'

Clare burst into wild laughter. 'She is your daughter, Robert, not a ship!' Looking at him now, pained and self-righteous, she felt a sudden lightness and knew that she had agreed to marry Mark to get out of this situation with Robert.

'I'm sorry, I really am — I did love you, I think — I was just rather stupid and didn't realize that a relationship like ours had the potential to become as stifling as a marriage — perhaps even more so.' She held out a hand to him. 'Can't we be friends still, Robert?'

'I think not.' He brushed past her and headed for the door. 'Goodbye, Clare — I hope you won't live to regret this.'

10

'Well, haven't you anything to say?' Clare demanded of Zoe. They were sitting opposite each other in the sandwich bar where they habitually lunched.

Zoe placed her salad roll down carefully on the plate in front of her. 'I think I am literally struck speechless,' she admitted.

'Then this must be a first,' Clare answered in a dry voice. Haltingly at first, then in a series of rushes, she had given her friend the bare bones of what was happening in her life. 'I thought you would be pleased at least, if not bursting to congratulate me. After all, you've lectured me enough about my relationship with Robert.'

'Too true!' Zoe nodded vigorously and mumbled the words through a large bite of her roll. 'I have to say I'm glad you've seen sense over that . . . ' she admitted after a few seconds of chewing and swallowing, 'but it does seem you have gone quite overboard by deciding to marry someone else,' She chuckled. 'Brilliant timing — just when he has finally decided to commit himself to you — because it suits him, of course. I would like to have been a fly on the wall when you told him. How did he take it?'

'Not particularly well. I can't say I really enjoyed telling him.' He had looked so hurt and amazed that Clare almost took back the words — might have done if he hadn't latched on to his explanation that she must have been leading a double life and two-timing him with Mark for some time. He had got quite abusive as his righteous indignation expanded to smooth his ego and had used such unpleasant language that he had merely hardened her resolve.

'Are you having an engagement party?' Zoe asked, staring at Clare with a sort of bemused admiration. She thought she must have fallen with a terrific bang to actually ditch Robert. It seemed very romantic to her. 'When is the big day? Soon, I hope . . . ' She rattled on without waiting for an answer. 'You can't afford to mess around for years — not at your age, not if you want kids — '

'I don't — at least I haven't even thought about it,' Clare cut in. She almost added that it was a most unlikely prospect as this marriage was strictly for convenience and business and, as Mark had said, would be 'in name only'. She looked at her friend, who was gazing at her, eyes bright with pleasure on her behalf, and knew that she would never, ever understand that — any more than she had been able to understand her long involvement with Robert. Zoe was a romantic at heart, as much now as when she had given up the prospect of a good career to marry and have children.

'There won't be time for an engagement party,' she told her now. 'We are getting married as soon as we can arrange it — you know, get the licence and all that.'

Zoe's eyes widened. 'You're not — are you pregnant?'

'No,' Clare almost snapped. 'No, it's just that — well, there is no point in messing about. We have a house and everything.'

'Does that mean you will be living in Maldon?'

'Of course not,' Clare retorted brusquely, then made a deliberate effort to soften her tone. 'I have no intention of giving up anything, certainly not my job, and commuting from Maldon would be a bit much. I shall keep my flat on and go on just the same — except for weekends. I'll probably spend those in Maldon.'

'Probably?' Zoe cut in. 'Of course you will. I should have thought you'd have moved up there altogether.' She wondered just what sort of a marriage this was going to be; to her it sounded very little better than the arrangement Clare had put up with from Robert for the last two years. 'Well, if you're not having an engagement party at least I can look forward to the wedding bash.' Zoe loved an excuse to celebrate — anything.

'I — I don't think there will be one. We're planning to just . . . well, just get married. Quietly, you know, just the two of us.'

'Well, for starters you can't do that — you have to have two witnesses. So you can count on me being there.' Zoe reached out and touched Clare's hand across the table, looking up and meeting her eyes. Clare was startled to see they were bright with the glint of unshed tears. Her voice was gravelly when she spoke. 'Clare, darling, you and I have been friends for so long you can't — you wouldn't think of getting married without me there, would you?'

Overcome with a sudden choking emotion, Clare could only shake her head, not trusting herself to speak as that was exactly what she had been planning. Zoe drew her hand away and sat back in her chair, looking at her, hurt puzzlement showing in her face.

'What's going on? What are you doing? Can't you tell me? No, don't if you really don't want to. I just hope you aren't jumping out of the frying pan into the fire. Tell me something about the guy anyway — obviously there is one!'

Haltingly Clare told her something about Mark and how she had spent the week working in the shop with him. She didn't explain the odd ramifications of the will but more by omission than what she said allowed Zoe to believe that instant passion had flared between them.

'Wouldn't it be prudent to wait a few months before you actually marry him?'

Clare shook her head, unwilling to admit the true reason for what seemed to Zoe such unseemly haste.

'Live with him for six months — see how you get on. You know, trial marriage.'

Clare shook her head. 'No — I — we don't want to do that.' She could see that her friend thought she was being unreasonable and foolish. She managed to smile. 'You can be a witness. You will, won't you?' she asked.

''Course I will. Mind you, I would much rather you had asked me to be matron of honour — but I promise I'll be there.'

★　★　★

There was no sign of Mark's car outside the cottage when Clare arrived mid-morning on the following Saturday so she drove round to the shop. To her surprise it was not only open but looked as if it were doing business. There

213

were buckets of bright gold Chrysanthemums glowing just inside the open door and more assorted flowers and plants in the shop than she had seen in the week she had worked there.

When she walked in, Mark was serving a customer. He looked up and she caught a look of surprise on his face; she couldn't be sure her arrival was a pleasant surprise or not till he smiled. For some reason this made her feel absurdly embarrassed and she turned away from him and gave her attention to the pot plants he had arranged at the side of the shop. She occupied herself in looking at them until the customer left the shop. Even then she found it hard to turn round and meet his eyes.

'Well, this is a surprise!'

'Not an unpleasant one, I hope?' Still unsure of her welcome, Clare took refuge in distance.

'Certainly not! In fact, I was going to call you this afternoon.'

'You were? What about?'

Mark raised his eyebrows. 'Well, what do you think? Unless of course you've had a change of h — mind.' He smiled broadly at her but Clare kept her voice cool.

'You don't have much faith in me. I thought I'd better come up and discuss the arrangements for our er . . . ' She floundered to a halt, quite unable to say the word wedding, finishing the sentence with the words 'business arrangement'.

'Ah yes, our business deal. You haven't changed your mind, then?' To Clare's supersensitive hearing, it seemed that he let a note of regret creep into his words.

'I'm not in the habit of changing my mind and reneging on arrangements, are you?'

'I am not.'

Clare looked round the shop and noted with both surprise and pleasure that several of the ideas and suggestions she had put forward during her days there had been implemented. She was startled when Mark said, 'Yes, you had some good ideas,' and not for the first time she wondered if he could read her mind. 'And I am not entirely close-minded.'

'Yes,' Clare muttered vaguely. 'The place looks good.' She sighed. 'You know I really enjoyed working here.'

'But you didn't stay.'

'I — I — well, no, I couldn't. I had a job to go back to.'

'Which no doubt you find much more enjoyable, more worthwhile?' Clare couldn't tell from his deadpan tone whether or not he was being sarcastic.

'Yes,' she said, much more firmly this time.

Mark just looked at her in silence. 'Of course,' he then said, his voice quite expressionless. He looked at his watch. 'It's almost midday. I think I've done all the trade I'm going to do today so how about I shut up shop and we go find something to eat?'

At the suggestion of food, Clare realized that she was actually quite hungry. Breakfast, which had only consisted of half a grapefruit, a slice of toast and a cup of coffee seemed a very long time back in the past. 'I'll help you,' she told him, and began fetching in the outdoor plants, straightening the shop and watering what needed watering, then finally sweeping up while Mark cashed up the till. It felt familiar — and good. She found that she was humming softly to herself as she worked.

'You really enjoy this place, don't you?' He sounded surprised.

Clare turned towards him, leaning on the broom handle. 'I enjoyed my week here,' she told him, implying that while a week was pleasant, for ever would not be.

Suddenly uncomfortable, she turned away from his gaze; she could feel he was still looking at her and hoped he hadn't noticed the flush of embarrassment warming her neck. When she turned back into the shop he had the cover on the cash register and was stashing the day's takings into his briefcase.

'Your place or mine?'

'Mine?' Clare was nonplussed.

'The cottage or your motel? I suppose you are here for the weekend.'

'Well — I — I, well — no.' She was blushing now in earnest. She hadn't thought further than seeing Mark to make the final arrangements for their marriage. She had simply got in the car and driven north.

'I guess it is mine, soon to be ours — in other words the cottage.' Mark's tone was dry but he was regarding her with a wry amusement that did nothing to restore her equilibrium. She followed him outside and got into her car while he locked the shop. She waited for him to move off first and then followed. As she drove she wondered if she had not, perhaps, taken leave of her senses after all. Then the cottage filled her vision and she felt again that strange sense of coming home. It filled her with a curious sense of peace, momentarily. But when she stepped out of her car and followed Mark to the door she wondered if maybe the wisest course of action would be to get back in her car, drive back to Melbourne and forget all about this utterly crazy course of action she had embarked upon.

'You had better get used to him,' Mark told

her as he led her through the back garden towards the back door. 'I could, of course, go through and let you in by the front door, but you can't avoid him for ever. After all, it is his house.'

Clare followed, silent and not a little apprehensive. Boris was so very large.

'He won't hurt you,' Mark told her, impatience tingeing his voice. 'He is actually very gentle.' He was right, of course; the huge dog reserved his exuberant pleasure for Mark, merely giving Clare a casual greeting, which, absurdly, made her feel almost neglected.

'Don't expect a feast,' Mark warned as he let them both into the house. 'Cheese and biscuits is about it.'

In actual fact his cheese and biscuits turned out to be bread rolls, salad and a wide range of cheeses. He turned to her from the open fridge. 'Beer?' he asked.

Clare nodded, and he brought out two cool lagers. When he had everything on the breakfast bar he drew up one of the pine stools and indicated the other opposite him. He took the caps off both bottles and pushed one over towards her. Clare poured it into her tumbler and took a long draft with the feeling that she was going to need it. She broke open a bread roll and helped herself to brie and salad. Only when they were both chewing in what, she had to admit, was a companionable way, did either of them speak; then it was in unison.

'Is everything arranged?' Mark asked.

Answering him before the question had registered, Clare told him, 'I think everything is organized. My friend Zoe will be a witness. Is there anyone special you want or do you want me to find a second person?'

'Timothy will be the other witness,' Mark told her laconically.

'Timothy? You mean Timothy Trimble?' Clare could not disguise her surprise at this choice.

'But of course.' He looked at her sharply. 'You haven't any objections, have you?'

'No — no, of course not, it's just that . . well, I just thought . . . no, that's OK.'

Mark raised his eyebrows. 'That's fine, then. I thought you sounded surprised.'

Clare mumbled a denial and took another gulp of the cool lager.

'It's not too late to back out, change your mind,' Mark surprised her by saying.

'In spite of what you said earlier?'

'In spite of what I said earlier.' He stared at her. Clare had the feeling that he was looking right into her — beyond her mind, even to her very soul — as she met, briefly, those vivid blue eyes before glancing down at her plate in confusion.

'No,' she mumbled. 'No, I don't want to back out.'

'Because of this house? Because you are so desperate to claim what you feel is yours, is that it?' There was a harsh, almost angry tone to his voice.

Clare looked up again and her voice was tight. 'Yes,' she told him.

Mark held her gaze for a moment, then sighed. 'I see. All the same . . . ' His voice trailed away and Clare heard the note of disappointment — with her, she supposed. She understood that for she felt much the same way herself. But when he spoke again she thought she must have imagined it, because his voice was brusque and business-like.

'In that case I think we should get down to brass tacks, the nitty-gritty. Work out just what we are going to do in a businesslike manner.' He pushed the remains of their meal to one end of the bench and reached for his briefcase. He fetched out a folder of printed pages and a large jotter pad together with a biro. On the top sheet he drew a vertical line down the centre of the page, dividing it into two columns. On one side he wrote her name, on the other his own.

'You want the house, this cottage, correct?'

Clare nodded, suddenly ashamed to be appearing so grasping and mercenary. 'And you want the business,' she supplied. 'But that hardly seems fair to me. This house is . . . well, it's lovely. The business is hardly even viable, it's more like a millstone. How are you going to make it pay?'

'You have forgotten the money.'

'Money? What money? I didn't even know there was any.'

'Well, not too much in actual cash as in money in the bank, but old Hester was a canny old bird and one of the things she was pretty cluey about is the stock market. She had a portfolio of about $200,000. More than enough to get the business up and running.'

Clare felt her jaw drop. 'Two hundred thousand?' she repeated.

'That's what I said. With that I can — '

'I'll say you can!' Clare interrupted, suddenly feeling as annoyed as if she had actually had the money in her hand and someone had snatched it from her. 'But this is the first I have heard about it! Why didn't you — why didn't someone tell me?'

'Why didn't you ask? Or at least take the trouble to read the will properly? You were so miffed about poor old Boris inheriting the house that you couldn't see beyond that.'

Clare stared at him. It was true. She had

not read the will properly. Even when Mark had given her a copy, she had stopped comprehending, as it were, when she came to all that about having to be married. Robert would have taken it all in. What had he said? Something about getting on to Timothy and getting things straight. She wondered if he had found out yet that she intended to marry Mark.

'What about all this?' She waved an expansive hand round the cottage.

'You mean the contents, furniture, etc? We can discuss this when we split up. I expect I will be generous; that is, if the shop is going really well.'

'I had forgotten we are not going to stay married,' Clare admitted, feeling a sudden hollow sense of loss at the thought.

'That — if you remember — was the plan, but as Robbie Burns so wisely said, 'The best laid plans of mice and men oft gang awry.''

As she met his eyes across the bench, Clare found a small smile was playing with the corner of her lips and there was a flame of hope somewhere inside her. 'Yes,' was all she said.

'Right, now let's get down to practicalities,' Mark said as he drew the jotter closer and began to write down things on either side of the vertical line.

'No doubt you will keep that 'who gets what' list in a safe place,' Clare remarked drily.

'Oh yes,' Mark agreed, 'We shall need it again when we part company.'

Clare felt anger and resentment flare. 'Look, I know this is a marriage of convenience and all that — even so, I wish you wouldn't keep harping on the ending of it when we haven't even begun it.'

'I'm sorry.' Mark looked genuinely surpised. 'I thought it would be reassuring for you to be reminded that you are not tying yourself up to me for life.'

'Hrrrumph.' Clare grunted vaguely and inelegantly, not sure how to respond.

'Are you going back to Melbourne tonight?' Mark asked, adding before she could answer, 'I suppose the next time we meet it will be to tie the knot.'

'I suppose,' Clare agreed.

'What part of my question were you answering?'

'Both — I think.'

'You don't have to go back tonight, you know,' Mark pointed out, adding, 'There is a spare bedroom here.'

'No — no I have to go.' She had been toying with the idea of staying overnight until he mentioned the spare bedroom. Not here, of course — in a motel. She couldn't have explained her feelings. She felt irrationally disappointed when Mark didn't try to persuade her to change her mind.

'I think we have everything organized now. We have both signed everything we need to sign and I have a celebrant lined up. Zoe insisted on having it at her house. We have been friends for so long she is like family — well, about the only family I have, really.'

'And the honeymoon? What about that?'

Clare looked up, startled. This was something she simply hadn't thought about.

'I . . . I . . . ' she stammered helplessly.

'I suppose you thought we could each just go to our separate homes and carry on as before?'

'No — I — well, yes, I suppose I did.'

'We shall both come back here and explain that as we are both so busy we are just having a couple of nights and we will take a proper honeymoon later on. That will be something to look forward to, won't it?'

Clare agreed, without thinking just what she was agreeing to, and found Mark grinning at her in obvious amusement.

'I never for one moment imagined that getting married like this would have so many complications,' she exclaimed. 'In fact I never ever thought my wedding would be like this.'

She spoke softly, almost to herself, and didn't realize just how wistful she sounded.

Mark threw her a swift glance but did not comment. Instead he merely muttered, somewhat irritatingly, 'Oh what a tangled web we weave . . . ' as he walked with her to her car. 'If you are sure you won't stay then I will look forward to seeing you in two weeks' time at the ceremony.' Clare nodded and was about to get in her car when he surprised her by gripping her tightly by each arm. 'There is just one thing, Clare. I want you to play fair with me.'

'Play fair?'

'Yes. We will be the only ones that know just what a sham our marriage really is and I shan't take kindly to being made a fool of, any more than if — '

'What are you talking about?' Clare wrenched herself free, rubbing her arms where he had gripped her.

'Finish with Robert — and don't let him know the truth.'

Clare gave a short mirthless laugh. 'That is over. Over, do you hear?' She scrambled into the driver's seat then wound down the passenger window and leaned across to hiss at him, 'But if it wasn't I should keep on just the same — if I wanted to.' Without giving him a chance to reply she zipped up the window and, releasing the handbrake was gone. It gave her some satisfaction to see him standing at the kerb with the cloud of dust she had raised settling round him, staring after her. Men, she thought. Everything had to be on their terms.

11

Back in her flat Clare stripped off and headed for the shower. She had found the journey stressful, not so much because of the actual driving but because of her thoughts, which seemed to whirl round her head. Not least was the niggling thought that maybe she was being unbelievably foolish. After all, what did she really know about Mark Fisk? Oh, she had liked him well enough when she had spent the week working in the shop, but to marry him — and for such a reason — maybe she had taken total leave of her senses. By the time she stepped out of the shower stall and wrapped a thick towelling robe round herself she had decided to call the whole crazy idea off. But before she could pick up the phone, her doorbell pealed.

Cursing softly to herself, Clare ran a comb through her damp hair and went to answer it.

'Robert!' Her first instinct was to slam the door in his face. But he had his hand on the open door and his foot in the gap.

'Can I come in, for a minute, please, Clare?'

Reluctantly she moved back and he

stepped quickly inside. 'Look, we have to talk — you can't just drop me like this.'

'I can and I have,' Clare said, but only inside her own head. Aloud she merely allowed her breath to escape in a sigh.

'Please, Clare . . . ' He stepped towards her and held out his arms, whether in supplication or intending to take her into them she wasn't sure. She stepped back and he let them drop to his sides again.

'Robert, it's over. I'm marrying someone else. I already told you that.' She saw a muscle throb in his cheek and a dark flush stain his skin.

'Yes, you told me, but I can't believe it.'

'Well, you had better because it is true,' she rapped back. She felt far too tired to even attempt to be soothing and tactful.

'It seems to me there are one of two things,' he went on as if she hadn't spoken. 'Either you've been two-timing me or you are marrying someone you can hardly know at all. If it's the first then I can only say I would never have believed that of you — if the second then, for the sake of all we meant to each other for so long, I beg you to think again.'

'Robert, I . . . ' she stammered, feeling herself weaken.

Seeing it, he grabbed her arms again and

begged, 'Tell me, how long have you known him! How long has this been going on?'

Anger, sharp and fierce, flared in Clare. 'I have already told you — it has not been going on at all till, well, till we decided to get married. As for how long I have known him — since I was a child — I met him then!' She stopped, aghast at her own manipulation of the truth. Mark had said he saw her as a child but that was hardly knowing and she for her part could not remember. But one thing was certain, she could never renew her relationship with Robert if he trusted her so little.

'Please go,' she said, moving towards the door.

'If you are marrying this whatever his name is just to pay me back then you are very foolish,' he told her, then, while Clare was still gaping at his ego, he paused at the door before flinging back at her, 'I hope you don't live to regret it!' The door slammed behind him and he was gone.

Left alone, Clare found she was shaking uncontrollably. In all the years she had known Robert she had never seen this side of him; it crossed her mind that maybe Linda had, which was why she had finally left him. But even more than that she was shocked and hurt at the accusations he had flung at her. She may be immature but surely not so childish to marry one man just to spite another, was she? Well, if nothing else Robert had made her mind up for her: whatever the outcome, there was no way she was going to back out of her arrangement with Mark now.

★ ★ ★

'But Clare, you only get married once. Well, most people do,' Zoe protested, leaning across the table in the café where they were lunching. 'You have to have some sort of a do — really. Let me arrange something at my place.'

Clare sighed. 'Oh, all right,' she reluctantly agreed. She was tired of the argument that had been an ongoing thing between Zoe and herself ever since she told her she was getting married in two weeks' time.

'I don't see what all the hurry is about. You say you aren't pregnant so — '

'Of course I'm not,' Clare snapped, amused in spite of herself at the mere suggestion and also noting that Zoe didn't appear to have noticed she had actually capitulated over the question of some sort of a reception. The argument had become such a part of life that Clare's change of answer passed by unnoticed, but only temporarily.

'Hey, did I hear right?' Zoe's hand stopped

halfway to her mouth, which was open to receive the salad roll it held. 'Did you actually agree to letting me do something for you?'

'You wore me down, but if you don't think you heard I can always — '

'Oh no you can't!' Zoe paused to chew vigorously for a few moments, gazing vaguely into the distance while her mind clacked over with ideas to make this low-key wedding Clare was insisting on memorable in some way. 'I think it would be nice if we had the whole thing at my place.' She turned back to Clare with a warm smile. 'We can have it in the garden, if you like. I always think a home wedding is — well, homely. Especially as you have got no family. What about Mark? Does he have a family?'

Clare looked blank. Had he? She didn't know — that was just another of the multiple things she was totally ignorant about. 'I — I don't know, I don't think so,' she stammered uncertainly.'

Zoe's eyebrows rose and she pursed her lips slightly. 'Gee, Clare, tell me something you do know about the guy!' Her voice was tart and when she saw the look of doubt and confusion on her friend's face she added in a softer tone, 'Look, tell me to shut up and mind my own business, if you like, but you really are sure you know what you are doing, aren't you?'

'I'm sure. And I won't tell you to mind your own business, although I admit I would like to, because I do realize that you care.' As she spoke Clare knew this was true and felt her throat constrict. In an unusual gesture of affection, she reached over and put her hand on Zoe's arm. 'I do appreciate it, really, and if you are quite sure you really want to take charge of my wedding then all I can say is thank you.'

Zoe grinned to hide her own emotion. 'Good. Now that's settled we can get down to brass tacks. First, what are you going to wear?'

'Wear?' Clare repeated blankly. She had given no thought to this at all. 'Oh, I'm sure I've got something that will do.'

'Clare Davenport — you are totally hopeless!' Zoe exclaimed. 'You have to have something special. No one ever gets married in some old thing that will do. We'll shop on Saturday morning.'

★   ★   ★

After nearly three hours of steady shopping, during which Clare had steadfastly rejected nearly every garment produced with 'Far too

232

fussy', 'I'd never wear that again', 'Much too expensive', 'No, no, NO. I am definitely NOT wearing white — or even cream!' and repeated reminders that this was to be a very, very quiet wedding, she finally settled on a light blue dress and matching jacket. Privately Clare still thought it a bit 'dressy', and doubted if she would ever wear it again, but at least it was not an exorbitant price, she felt comfortable in it and knew it suited her. Best of all, by its purchase the subject of what she would wear was settled to Zoe's satisfaction and even more or less to her own.

Not caring to spend the next two weeks in a non-stop verbal battle with her friend, Clare gave in — if not graciously then at least without too much argument — over the details of the other wedding arrangements. She found it necessary to call Mark on more than one occasion to ask him who he wanted to ask to the wedding and check other details.

'Oh, just old Tim,' he said casually. 'I can't think of anyone else who would be the least interested. The only two who might can't be asked.'

'Why not?'

'Well, one is dead — I would have loved dear old Hester to have been there — and the other . . . well, I don't think he would be a suitable guest.'

'Well, ask him anyway,' Clare urged, feeling that this whole wretched affair was rapidly becoming her party. 'Give me his address and I'll see he gets an invitation. There's still time to post one.'

'No, forget it — he can't read anyway.'

'Oh,' was all Clare could find to say here, wondering whether this person was either a small child or someone illiterate.

'Dogs can't usually,' Mark added and laughed, 'but I would dearly love to have old Boris there. After all, without him there wouldn't be a wedding.'

'Bring the damn dog then, if you really want him. I don't suppose he can do any harm,' Clare snapped, irritated at the way she had been concerned about Mark having no-one to ask. It occurred to her that this was much how Zoe must have felt about herself.

This exchange had slipped into the realm of past and forgotten conversations when the Saturday morning of their marriage rolled inexorably round. That being so, she was surprised when she heard an exclamation from Zoe, who was looking out of the window at the time, hoping to get a glimpse of the other party to this strange marriage.

'What the — ' she spluttered suddenly. 'Some idiot is just coming up the garden path with a monster. Actually, I think it is a dog

— but it's about the biggest I've ever seen!'

'White and black, hairy, long legs and long nose?' Clare ventured.

'You know it? And the man?' Zoe asked fearfully.

'Mark and Boris,' Clare observed stoically.

'And which is which? I mean, which is the one you are marrying?'

'The man, of course!' Clare snapped, adding with a deep sigh of resignation, 'I said for him to bring Boris if he wanted but I didn't mean it.'

'There's another car drawn up and another man is getting out. Ah, this one appears to be sane. No monster with him anyway. They seem to be arguing and now they are both marching off — dog as well.'

'They are probably just taking him for a walk,' Clare told her. 'Stop your running commentary at the window and come and help me get ready.'

'I thought you were ready — such as it is. Just putting on that dress isn't too difficult, surely? No long train, no veil to adjust, no bridesmaids to make sure they are dressed correctly . . . No flowers even!' Zoe could not reconcile herself to what she called Clare's utility wedding.

'There will be no wedding either if you don't stop nagging. Just look at me and tell me if I look — well, all right.' Clare felt overcome with a sense of total unreality. Was this really her wedding day? Nothing could have been further from any girl's dream — and she had once dreamed. Had she really agreed to go through with this crazy farce? She stared at her face in the mirror — it stared back at her, white and strained, and she swung round to face Zoe. 'It's no good. I can't go through with it!'

Zoe turned back into the room and met Clare's eyes in the mirror. For a moment she was taken aback by the bleakness she saw there and the panic-stricken white face. But she wasn't about to allow sympathy to engulf her; if she did Clare probably would go to pieces completely. Zoe had come to the conclusion that almost any marriage to anyone was an improvement on the entanglement Robert had kept her in for the last couple of years — years thrown away, wasted. Quickly she left the room and came back with a shot of brandy and handed it to Clare with the admonition, 'Drink that — and don't argue!'

Clare, spluttering as the fiery liquid hit her throat, couldn't speak, let alone argue. She took the next sip more slowly. 'You are supposed to help me dress and give me moral support, not get me paralytic,' she complained, but her last words were drowned by the chiming of Zoe's very noisy doorbell. There was a clatter and a scuffle then her teenage son stuck his head round the door to announce that the celebrant was here and two men and a big dog were walking up the garden path.

'That's the bridegroom,' Zoe told him, to which she got the inevitable question:

'Which one? Is it the dog?'

'That's enough teenage humour for one day,' she admonished her son. 'Let them in — well, the men anyway. See if you can get them to put the dog in the car or something.'

A few seconds later he was back. 'He's wearing a big white bow, and one of the men says he is a guest at the wedding — that Clare specifically invited him.' He was grinning from ear to ear — what had looked like being a very dull business was looking up.

'Of course I didn't!' Clare stormed, indignation and brandy bringing some colour to her cheeks. 'Well, that's to say, I did, but I didn't mean it . . . Oh, come on — let's get on with this damn wedding. It seems everyone is here.' She stomped out of the bedroom and headed for Zoe's lounge, looking more like an avenging angel than a bride. Zoe, with a shrug, hastily followed her.

In an incredibly short time, it seemed to Clare, who was feeling strangely out of it, thanks in part to Zoe's brandy, she and Mark were married. Zoe, her husband and children, Timothy and Boris were witness to it. The dog, to her enormous relief, sat still where he was told, no doubt subdued by the indignity of wearing a large white satin bow. Clare, feeling as if she wasn't quite there, looked vaguely round when Mark was told by the celebrant that he could kiss the bride. With a shock she realized that she was the bride and obediently turned her face to Mark to receive his kiss.

She had to admit that she quite enjoyed the little party afterwards. Zoe, who was a great cook and loved an opportunity to show off her skill, had prepared a delicious light buffet lunch, laid on bottles of champagne and even ordered a cake. She was determined that however small the wedding there was no way she was not going to be sure that Clare had a good send-off.

'Thank you — it's been marvellous. You have been wonderful!' Clare hugged her friend as they made ready to leave. 'I'll see you on Monday.'

'Monday! Surely you aren't planning to be back in the office then? What about your honeymoon?'

'No honeymoon.' Clare tried to sound casual but seeing Zoe's expression added, 'Yet.'

'But you must have a honeymoon!' Zoe, a staunch traditionalist, protested. 'We aren't so busy we can't manage without you.'

'We're going away later on. We're just going back to the house — home.' She added the last word as a rather belated after-thought.

Zoe stared at her, then hugged her tightly and in an odd thick voice muttered, 'Be happy — whatever you do!'

'Take me round to my flat, please,' Clare said as she got into the passenger seat beside Mark.

'Your flat? But I thought — well, we are married now . . . surely you're going to spend some time in the cottage?' His voice trailed away, he had been going to add something about the place she had gone to such lengths to get.

'Mark,' Clare spoke in the patient tones of someone explaining the very simple and obvious to a very stupid listener, 'Mark, I have to get back to Melbourne to work on Monday morning. To do that I shall need my car. So please take me to my flat so that I can collect it.'

He watched her go inside and come out carrying a small suitcase, a briefcase and a laptop. This looked like being a great honeymoon weekend, he reflected somewhat gloomily. In spite of everything he had, foolishly no doubt, expected a bit more.

'You can go on,' Clare told him. 'I know the way.' She got into her car and slammed the door shut, but not before Mark had managed to say, 'Funny wedding — when the bride and groom leave in different cars.' He watched her start off then leaned over into the back seat and ripped off the satin bow round Boris's neck. Dammit, he thought, if he had anywhere to go he would go there! He should have come down in Timothy's car — would have done if he had an inkling that he and Clare would be leaving separately.

Heading north, Clare was sorely tempted to just keep on driving out of this totally absurd situation she had put herself in. The only thing that kept her car heading for Maldon was that she had somewhere to go there — and on reflection it didn't seem practical or even possible to actually drive away from her life. But she did find that she was driving rather slowly, the result being that Mark was at the cottage long before her. She pulled up outside the house and gazed at it, telling herself it was now hers — or would be very soon. She waited for some reaction in herself: pleasure, even elation. None came and with a sigh she got wearily out of the car and unlatched the garden gate.

Mark must have seen her arrive, probably wondered why she was sitting so long in the car. He opened the door just as she reached it and to her alarm snatched her up bodily from the ground.

'What are you doing? Put me down!' she screeched, drumming her heels against him. He dropped her just inside and pushed the door shut behind them.

'Whatever do you think you are doing?' she demanded again. 'Have you gone out of your mind? I was scared to death.' He just stood looking at her, grinning foolishly, and she realized he was just following tradition and carrying his bride over the threshold. To her fury she felt hot colour flooding not only her cheeks but her whole body. Turning her back on him she marched into the house, calling back over her shoulder, 'Where shall I put my things?'

'In the bedroom, I guess.'

'Which bedroom?'

'Well, that depends, doesn't it? The one with the double bed in it is mine — the one with the single bed the spare room. Take your pick.'

'I will,' Clare retorted and flung open both doors before throwing her case down firmly on the single bed. If he thought there were going to be any more traditional bridal goings-on then he was very wrong, she told herself. Mark watched, shrugged and turned away.

'Would you like to go out for a meal?' he asked, in a tight voice.

'No,' Clare answered shortly, adding a belated, 'Thanks. I'm too tired. It's been a big day.' As soon as she had spoken she wished the words unsaid. It was true, of course — wedding days usually were — but this had been no ordinary wedding.

Mark simply shrugged and turned back into the kitchen and began stoically preparing a meal. Clare looked at his back for a moment, suppressing an urge to walk up behind him and put her arms round him. Instead she went into the bedroom, pulled the case towards her that she had unceremoniously thrown on to the bed, and unpacked the things she would need for the weekend.

It was an uncomfortable meal. Neither of them were hungry and conversation was polite and stilted between them. Mark made coffee and without consulting her poured a whisky for both of them. 'I think you need this,' he told her, 'and I'm sure I do. We have to talk, Clare, and now seems as good a time as any.'

'I'm tired — I told you. And I don't want that.' She pushed the whisky away from her and the coffee towards her.

'I think you do, you know,' Mark said quietly, pushing it back across the counter in her direction. 'And we do have to talk — putting it off won't make it any easier.'

Clare stared at him, reached for the whisky glass and took such a large gulp she gasped. After a few minutes' silence, Mark said softly, 'I'm sorry. I guess I have made rather a fool of myself. I honestly thought this was a good idea and when you agreed to it I thought you did too. I even thought you didn't mind the idea — that you didn't mind me. I see I was wrong and I'm sorry. I won't hold you to any silly agreement. I'll pack up over the weekend and clear out, if that will help?'

Her initial reaction was, Yes, yes, wonderful, then she remembered: 'And Boris — will you take him?'

'Oh God, I forgot about Boris.' Mark stared at her across the counter and when she raised her eyes to his, Clare was astonished to see that he looked hurt and bewildered more than angry. It took the edge off. She found her own anger had dissolved, leaving only a feeling of depression and failure in its place.

'I'll send for him when I've got somewhere to keep him,' he finally muttered.

'Keep him at the shop,' Clare snapped.

'But I shan't be at the shop. Haven't you understood at all? I said I would leave — get out of your house, your life and your shop.'

'But that's not fair! I mean, the agreement was that the business was yours — '

'Of course it's not fair!' With an angry gesture he tilted his own whisky glass and drank most of the contents in one go. 'But since you have made it painfully obvious — not just now but all day — that you can't stand either of us, Boris or me, then I will go. I will come back for him as soon as I have found a place to live with him!'

'You can't do that. You can't leave me here with . . . with that dog. What will I do on Monday morning when I have to go back to Melbourne?'

'I don't care what you do. I'm just reminding you who really owns this place: not me, not you, but Boris. I thought you were just nervous earlier on and made allowances, stupid of me. You, my dear Miss Davenport, are not the only person round here who has made a terrible mistake.' He pushed back the bar stool he was perched on and stood, glaring at her. 'But at least I was prepared to honour our arrangement, and I am not,' he added, 'talking about anything but practical matters. If you think for one moment that I was considering demanding anything else from this bloody marriage you are wrong, very wrong. I have not — never have had — the slightest intention of raping you!'

Clare felt he had stopped just short of saying that he had no desire to either when he turned round at the door and added in icy tones, 'There is a lock, with a key in it, on your bedroom door. I suggest you use it as you have so little confidence in me.' He made to go then hesitated and turned again. 'We will talk in the morning to arrange the practical side of our separation.' The last word was spat out with irony and Clare found herself alone, staring at the space where he had been and listening to the relatively quiet but quite definite slam of his door.

She cleared up their few dishes, intending to merely pile them on the draining board, then overcome by a shaft of guilt she turned on the tap and washed them. The small task was therapeutic; at least she felt marginally better about things when she crept into her own bed. She fully expected to toss through a sleepless night and was astonished to open her eyes to see sunlight streaming in through the window. In her exhaustion the previous evening, she had not drawn the curtains.

Clare slid out of bed, and a glance at her watch told her that it was just after eight o'clock. She padded over to the window which overlooked the back yard; Boris was out there looking expectantly at the back door. As she watched it was opened, and with his plume of a tail waving his appreciation the great animal trotted into the house. Making a mental note not to allow such familiarity if he was to be left with her, Clare looked round for her slippers. When she remembered she had not brought them, she pushed her arms into the sleeves of the thin summer robe she had brought, yanked the belt tight with a viciousness that caused her to catch her breath, and left her room and headed in the direction of the kitchen. She opened the door in time to see Mark pass the great animal a slice of rather well-done toast.

Clare hesitated for a moment in the doorway. Boris gave her a cursory glance then turned his attention back to Mark and the toast. She advanced cautiously into the room and pulling out a stool on the opposite side of the bench to the dog, perched on it with her bare feet tucked up under the folds of her robe.

'I . . . I'm sorry about last night,' she mumbled. 'I guess you're right. We do have to talk. We've got to work out something about this crazy situation we seem to have landed ourselves in.'

Mark looked at her for a moment, gauging how genuine her change of tone was. 'Tea or coffee?' was all he said.

'Coffee, please,' Clare answered automatically, then seeing a thin spiral of smoke rising from the toaster suggested, 'Shouldn't you turn that thing down?'

Throwing her a look she couldn't quite fathom, Mark did as she suggested. He removed two more slices of decidedly well-done toast, and looking at them critically once more passed them to Boris.

'You could always scrape them,' Clare could not resist pointing out.

'I could but I choose not to. Anyway, Boris doesn't mind.'

'I suppose he wouldn't get them if they were perfectly done?' Clare hazarded.

'Probably not,' Mark replied vaguely before passing her across a large mug of steaming coffee. He pushed sugar and milk in its wake, removed two perfectly done slices from the toaster, dropped in a couple more then sat down on the stool opposite her.

'What time do you plan to leave?'

'Leave?' Clare, absently stirring her coffee, was startled by the question. 'Oh yes, well . . . ' She stopped in some confusion remembering their conversation of the previous evening. 'Would you mind — I mean, have you any objection to me staying for another night?' she asked tentatively.

Mark grinned. 'I guess you *would* look pretty silly arriving home the morning after your wedding. I can just see the headlines: '*Bride runs away from honeymoon.*''

'Nothing of the sort,' Clare expostulated indignantly, then seeing the grin on his face admitted, 'Oh, all right then, I admit I would look pretty silly, but I would really like to stay if I may. After all, we have a lot of talking to do.' To her own great surprise, Clare found she really meant it: she did want to stay and not, if she was totally honest, just to talk.

Neither spoke for a few minutes; the only sound was the homely companionable noises of two people eating breakfast together. Boris sat looking at them then, with a deep sigh, when he saw no more toast seemed to be forthcoming, he flopped down on the floor taking up almost the entire space. Mark slid off his stool. 'OK, old man, now you've had brekkie I think you can go out.' With another sigh and a reproachful glance over at Clare as if he blamed her for his banishment, the huge dog obediently trotted out through the door that Mark had opened for him.

Clare finished her toast and pushed her plate away, then, suddenly very much aware of her state of undress, she got down abruptly from her stool. 'I'll go and put some clothes on,' she told Mark in a rather tight voice as she left the room. 'May I have a shower?' She put her head back round the door.

'Go for your life — whose shower is it anyway?'

'I meant . . . ' she began, meaning to add that she just wondered about hot water, but there was something about his back view that made her close first her mouth and then the door.

She didn't hurry over her shower; instead she allowed herself to enjoy the delicious sensation of warm water running down her face and over her body, a sensation that was both relaxing and revitalizing. When she finally towelled herself dry she felt ready to face anything — and anyone.

Mark was not in the kitchen; she found him sitting out in the back yard, lolling in a garden chair. A thin curl of smoke rose from the fingers of his right hand and she saw that he was smoking.

'I didn't know you — ' she began as she dropped into the chair on the opposite side of the small garden table.

'I don't,' he almost snapped. 'Only in moments of crisis.'

'Is this one?' Clare asked quietly.

He stared at her for a moment. 'No!' he

said abruptly and, dropping the glowing cigarette on the flagstones, ground it out viciously. 'Do you think it is?'

Not sure how to answer, Clare merely shrugged. As the silence dragged out she murmured hesitantly, 'I thought you wanted to talk?'

'No,' he rasped, just when she thought he wasn't going to answer. 'I want you to talk. I want to know just why you agreed to marry me, made no attempt to get out of it while there was still time, before it was a fait accompli, and now, after the event, act like some outraged virgin that has been kidnapped by white slavers or something. I want an explanation, Clare — I feel you owe me that at least. You seemed to think it was a tolerable if not actually brilliant idea when I first mooted it' He stopped and stared at her and she, helplessly, stared back. Unable to find words to answer him, she shook her head mutely.

'Oh, come on, say something. I'm disappointed in you — I had hoped for a good business arrangement, even some lively arguments. I never thought you'd run out on me quite so soon. But just do me one favour. Please tell me why you agreed to marry me in the first place.'

'I suppose I was tempted. This cottage, I

love it so, and my aunt did leave it to me, and I've never really had a home — certainly never actually owned a house. Oh, I'm sorry, I really am, I know I have been quite horribly unfair to you. I suppose all I can truly say is I was tempted, and I fell.'

'Well, I can understand that. It is your house, by rights. If old Hester hadn't left such a daft will you would probably have been installed by now and I would have been out on my ear — we both would.'

'Both?'

He nodded at the dog. 'Him and me.'

Clare followed his gaze and in all honesty could only agree. 'Yes, well . . . ' She tried to stifle the sudden twinge of guilt. 'She did leave a will full of clauses and things and here we all are — so it seems to me we'd better make the best of it.'

'Isn't that exactly what I was trying to do when I suggested this marriage thing?' Mark leaned towards her, and Clare found herself suddenly unable to face the challenge in those brilliant blue eyes. Then he leaned back in his chair and shot at her, 'What exactly did you mean when you said that about never having a home? You had one when I first met you — as a child, I mean — all those years ago.'

Clare nodded. 'I lost it immediately after

that. My father left my mother, went back to England; there were a few years with my mother, just the two of us. But she wasn't much good at home-making. We kept moving into one rented place then another, then she finally married one of the 'uncles' that came in and out of our lives. I thought things might be better. I didn't mind Joe — in fact, he had always been quite nice to me — but that was when I wasn't his responsibility in any way. After he married Mum he seemed to resent me and kept asking why my father didn't have me: 'Take responsibility for his own bloody kid,' was the way he put it. Then she was killed — a car crash — and of course he wanted me even less then. He got on to my father in England and told him to come and get me. I didn't mind at the time — in fact, I had all sorts of romantic ideas about being reunited with my sweet, kind, loving father — and how there would be just the two of us . . . ' Her voice trailed away on a sound that sounded as if it might easily break into a sob.

'And it wasn't like that?' Mark asked softly.

Clare shook her head. 'It wasn't like that at all. No one had told me my father had married again and that he already had another daughter and another baby on the way. No one wanted me, least of all my stepmother.' Clare paused, letting her thoughts take her back to that dreadful unhappy time when she had felt totally deserted and rejected.

To Mark listening, and watching, it seemed that she actually shrank, wilted certainly, with the memory of the bleak years behind her. He longed to reach across the table and take her hand. More, he would have liked to get up and put his arms round her; he was astonished at the strength of his need to comfort her and with an effort condensed his feelings into what came out as little more than a sympathetic grunt. He wanted to ask what had happened then — how had that unhappy, damaged child managed to become the attractive and successful woman that she was today?

'And Robert? Where did you meet him?'

'I went to a legal conference — Robert was there. He gave me a lift home.'

Mark thought he could see it all clearly: the older man, successful in his own profession, young enough to play Prince Charming, old enough to be a father figure.

'What made you get involved with him? Did you know he was married?'

Clare nodded. 'He never made any secret of it. I didn't mind at first — in fact, I was quite glad. What I've seen of marriage it didn't look such a good option. Then I suppose I got clucky or something — or tired of just being 'the other woman'.'

'The one who spends Christmas Day alone.'

Clare smiled. 'Something like that, except that I didn't spend Christmas Day alone. Zoe was always a good friend and saw to that.'

'Yes, I liked her, and I could see how much she cared about you.'

'I thought when my relationship with Robert began that it was perfect. I was quite cynical about marriage in general. I didn't think it was for me: I couldn't visualize ever willingly getting tied to another person for ever. Marriage, I had decided, was definitely not for me. Personally I doubted if it was for anyone.'

'So you put your knowledge into busting up other people's marriages? You became a divorce lawyer.'

'Yes, it does seem like that,' Clare admitted, 'then something changed. Maybe I was just ageing. Things stopped being so clear cut; I began to think wistfully about a home of my own. I didn't feel so good about my job any more. I told myself I was getting soft in the head.' She smiled self deprecatingly.

Mark shook his head. 'Not soft in the head. Just allowing the true softness of your heart to surface,' he told her gently.

Clare looked up at him in surprise; she had almost forgotten he was there as she talked. She had voiced aloud things she had hardly dare admit to herself before. It had been a therapeutic experience.

'I can understand now how important this cottage is to you — a home of your own, and coming to you from your own family.'

'Yes. I — I guess so,' Clare said in a rather tight little voice.

Mark stood up abruptly. 'I'm going to get a paper. Come on!'

Clare almost got up too, then realized it was the dog, not her, he was inviting to accompany him. She sat back in her seat and felt the old, familiar sense of rejection settle round her heart. Why on earth, she wondered, had she told him all that, things she never talked about to anyone?

12

Mark and the big dog walked for hours. Or so it seemed. He was almost as surprised as Clare that she had confided in him, and not sure he was pleased. He had thought he was beyond emotions, caring for people, being hurt empathetically, yet, listening to her story he had found himself feeling not just for her but with her. He had thought this marriage was an excellent way to repay Hester without involving himself. It didn't seem to be turning out that way.

When he finally got back to the house he found Clare in the kitchen. As far as he could see she was preparing a meal, just like any housewife, and just like any wife she turned round with a 'Hi! Enjoyed your walk?' She glanced fleetingly at his hand but neither of them mentioned the fact that there was no newspaper in it. 'If you want to eat, the meal will be ready in about fifteen minutes.'

'Time for a shower?'

'Oh, yes, plenty,' Clare assured him before turning back to stir something on the stove top.

'Is that pasta?' Mark asked as he came back

to the kitchen, fresh from his shower.

'Yes — do you mind?! It was all I could find in the pantry cupboard and the fridge.'

'Not at all — I love it. I was just asking to see what wine I should dig out to go with it.'

'Oh,' Clare murmured. He seemed to have a good cache of wine stuffed away here in the cottage.

'Hester always kept a good cellar,' Mark told her, as if reading her thoughts. 'She was actually quite a wine buff and taught me what little I know. So I think a nice mellow red with pasta; there is a genuine Italian Lambrusco tucked away somewhere.'

While he busied himself finding and uncorking the bottle, Clare served the meal. She half smiled to herself wondering how they had managed to reach this state of gentle domesticity after the somewhat turbulent start to their weekend.

'I'm sorry I unburdened myself on you like that.' Clare finally broke the silence as they sat opposite each other.

'No need to be sorry. I am flattered that you told me.' Mark paused, frowning slightly and pushing his food round on his plate so that Clare thought there was something he didn't like about it. Seeing her watching him he said quickly, 'It's very good — it is my thoughts that I don't care for.'

'Why think them then?' Clare retorted flippantly.

'You made me. Telling me so much about yourself you made me feel, well, guilty, I suppose — that I'd told you so little about myself and expected you to marry me.'

'Well, yes, but do I need to know as this marriage of ours is hardly likely to be a long-lasting one?'

'True.' He shrugged. 'Well, the truth is you would probably have turned the whole idea down flat if you had known a bit more about me.'

'As I don't know, I can't say whether I would or not.' Clare looked straight at him and their eyes met in a searching stare. She was the first to lower hers. 'But I can't believe there is anything so bad. I can usually rely on my own judgement.'

'Like you did with Robert?'

Clare flushed. 'Yes, like I did with Robert,' she retorted defiantly. 'He was always kind and considerate. Our relationship lasted two years; it was just what I wanted, what I needed at the time. I didn't want marriage, I didn't want ties, but I did need to feel that I was, well, attractive, I suppose. I needed to feel wanted. He gave me all that. I think the trouble lay more with me than him. Suddenly it wasn't enough for me.'

'But he told you his wife was leaving him — he was free then to marry you. Why did you change your mind?'

Clare, looking at him, might have answered, 'Because I met you.' For that was the thought that flashed to mind. She dismissed it instantly as absurd, knowing that she couldn't say that — and anyway it simply was not true, was it? It was her turn to shrug dismissively now. 'Sheer cussedness, probably.' She had revealed enough of herself without going into the complex feelings she had for Robert, most of which she scarcely understood herself. 'Look,' she said now, 'we've got ourselves into what I, for one, am beginning to feel is a rather crazy situation. We need to talk sensibly, decide what we are going to do in a practical way, and I think you and the shop are the most important. What we are going to do with it; what *you* want to do. If you are serious about making it into a going concern, then we need to work out ways and means.'

'And you?' Mark asked quietly. 'What are you going to do?'

'Me? Oh, I shall go on as before. I shall continue to live in my little apartment in Melbourne and go to my office and spend my days 'busting up other people's marriages', as you so nicely put it. The problem is the weekends. It will look so odd if I stay there all

259

week so soon after our wedding, so if you have no objection, I'll come up here and help you with the shop.' She paused for a moment to remember, then, 'You know, Mark, I really enjoyed that time I spent in it. I — ' She had been going to say that she wouldn't mind doing it full-time, but stopped abruptly. After all, the terms of their agreement were that the shop was his.

'But I shall be living in your house.'

'That's different; you have to do that to look after Boris. I think,' she added after a pause, 'that we should get our heads together and see what can be done about the shop. I brought my computer along with me so that we can get some sort of a plan down.'

'I've already done that.'

'You have? But I thought — I mean, when I was up here helping you, I suggested a computer and . . . well I'm not sure what you said but I can't remember you were very enthusiastic.'

'That was then, this is now,' he commented somewhat enigmatically. 'If you care to come into my bedroom.'

'Your bedroom?' Clare echoed, wondering if this was a variant on 'Come into my parlour said the spider to the fly'.

Mark grinned, and she had a horrible suspicion that he was reading her thoughts yet again. 'I keep my computer there.'

'Of course.' Clare murmured, feeling both foolish and naïve.

After she had been standing behind him, trying to follow what he was doing on the screen for some time, she looked around for another seat. The only one seemed to be an upright chair with a pile of his clothes thrown over it in haphazard abandon.

'Just chuck them off!' he told her. 'Either that or fetch a chair in from the lounge.'

Clare was about to do just that then, looking at the chair so close at hand, she thought, no, how absurd to be affected by that pile of clothing lying on the only chair in the room. She snatched up the clothes in one arm and chucked them casually on to the bed, which was, she couldn't help but notice, a double one. As she did she caught a whiff of male scent, mostly perspiration it was true, but there were other outdoorsy smells mixed up in it. As she turned round to move the freed chair closer to the computer, she was aware that Mark was watching her. He turned back quickly to the flickering screen, but not before their eyes had met in a swift, electrifying flash. As nonchalantly as she could, Clare drew the chair up beside him.

'So what's this?' she asked, nodding at the list on the screen.

'Oh, nothing much, just some ideas I drew up for improving the shop.' With a click the list disappeared.

'Oh, no, turn back, please!' Clare begged. 'I was in the middle of reading that. I was interested; I thought there were some really good ideas there.' She began reading through them half aloud, interjecting comments as her eyes travelled down the screen.

'Hmm, yes, I think that is definitely a good idea.' She paused and turned towards him to find herself looking directly into his face, which was turned towards her. 'It does need a lick of paint,' she said quickly to hide her confusion.

'I was thinking of rather more than a lick of paint. In fact I was considering a complete makeover.' His attention was back on the screen now.

'But won't that be costly — in time as well as materials?'

'Probably — but necessary I feel. It is so dull and dowdy that it would take cartloads of expensive flowers to make it look even moderately bright and cheerful.'

Clare smiled slightly; he was exaggerating, of course, but he was also right.

'But the money — it would cost an awful lot to do all these things you have suggested here. Is it going to be worth it and have you got that sort of money?'

'The answer to both those questions is yes,' he replied tersely.

'Good.' Clare's reply was equally terse. 'But what about time?'

'Yes, that is more of a difficulty. I should have to shut, of course, and every day closed is a loss of business. But obviously there is no way I could get the structural improvements done and paint the whole place in less than a week at the very quickest.'

'More like two, or at least ten days.' Clare could not resist saying, 'On the other hand . . . ' She paused, afraid that she was maybe saying too much.

'On the other hand?' Mark encouraged, then finished her sentence off himself. 'On the other hand, if I don't do it now while the shop is so run down, hardly any stock or fittings, it will be much, much harder to do it later on.'

'So?'

'So I guess I will do it now,' he said decisively.

'Oh Mark, it will look terrific. I can just see it. You've got some great ideas: it looks about twice as big here.' She had clicked on to a simulation he had done of the finished shop; the concrete floor had a pattern of flowers painted on it and the walls were done in brilliant colours. 'These walls look really good, but . . . ' she hesitated before saying tentatively, 'Wouldn't flowers with their own bright colours show up better on white?'

'I thought of that. But I want something different.' He thought for a moment. 'How about black?'

'Black!' Clare echoed. Then she closed her eyes and thought, visualizing a bank of brilliantly coloured flowers against a black background. 'Do you know, I think that would work, I do really. You could have a coloured ceiling, gold or something, like the sun, good lighting — and how about a big mirror on one wall reflecting the flowers?' She paused, almost out of breath. 'That would give customers the impression you had double the stock.' She laughed. 'Oh, Mark, you can make it great — I know you can!'

'I think so too. Especially with your input. You have some really good ideas, Clare. Thanks!'

'But the original idea of black walls was yours,' she reminded him, turning to look at him, her eyes shining with enthusiasm, her cheeks faintly flushed. Mark stared at her then got up abruptly and began striding about the room.

Clare suddenly felt deflated. Had she annoyed him with her suggestions? Had he felt she was interfering? She too got up and made for the door. 'Sorry,' she mumbled, gasping as he gripped her arm.

'What the hell are you sorry for? You've given me some brilliant ideas. I just can't wait to start doing something about it.'

'Why do you have to wait? What's wrong with now?' Clare surprised herself by demanding. 'Come on, let's go and look at it. We can plan better if we are actually there, in the place.'

★   ★   ★

In the shop, they stood together looking round. At first Clare found she could only remember the happy hours she had spent in here, then as they began to talk and plan she found she was being taken over by an enthusiasm that almost amounted to excitement.

'There is a lot of junk needs throwing out,' Mark remarked rather glumly, 'before we can even start work on the place.'

Clare noticed the 'we' and wondered who he was referring to. 'Have you got someone to help you?' she asked.

'No. Why?' Then he realized. 'I said 'we', didn't I? I should have remembered and said 'me' but I suppose that makes the whole project seem a bit daunting.' His voice trailed off as he visualized doing all this on his own.

Clare was silent — she was visualizing the same thing. After a long silence, while they both were absorbed in their own thoughts, Clare tentatively suggested, 'I could — But no, you probably wouldn't want that. I could stay on a bit and help — that is, if you thought I could — if you wanted me.'

Mark was silent for so long that Clare thought either he hadn't heard, or more likely had heard and rejected the suggestion. She was actually turning away as if to leave when he said, 'Do you mean that, Clare? You're not having me on?'

'Of course I mean it. If you wanted me and thought I could help, I can stay on for a few days, maybe a week.'

'But I thought you had to get back?'

Clare had the grace to blush. 'Well, not really. Actually, I have nothing on this week that can't either wait or be dealt with by Zoe.'

'I think I'm dreaming but if I'm not, or even if I am, let's get started! We can at least clear out some of this rubbish, make a start, clear the decks so that we can get really stuck into it Monday morning.'

'Tomorrow,' Clare pointed out with a smile.

There was a strong feeling of déjà vu about the next few days, for Clare at any rate. Working side by side with Mark in the shop reminded her of the short time she had spent as his assistant. It was a daunting task; the entire first day was spent clearing out the junk and rubbish and scraping down and cleaning the walls ready for painting.

As she scrubbed, a thought occurred to Clare. 'Mark, who does this shop belong to?'

'What sort of a silly question is that?'

'No, it's not silly. There are two parts to a business, as you well know — the actual business itself and the premises that house it. I know the business was Hester's but what about this building?'

'Well, it belonged to Hester, of course. She would have no truck with paying rent and when this place came on the market she bought it.'

'You mean she bought the premises to house the shop?'

'That's right. There was already a shop of sorts here. An untidy little second-hand place, well, a junk shop, really. It was only open on high days and by days and when the old man who ran it died it never opened again.'

'Did Hester run the flower shop herself?'

'More or less. She tried to.'

267

'What do you mean, tried to? From what I have heard of her she was a person who did things, not who tried to.'

'You're quite right there.' Mark sighed and for a moment Clare thought that was all the explanation she was going to get, then, 'I guess she had left her run to be a shopkeeper just too late. She had barely opened when she was diagnosed with terminal cancer. That's when she should have sent for me — or I should have come. But she was stubborn, and proud, so by the time I got here it was too late.'

'I see,' Clare murmured soothingly. She didn't really but was unwilling to say anything that might stem this flow of data. She had found it so hard to get any real information from anyone about this woman who she had never really known but who had, incredibly, changed her entire life.

'When I finally got here I found the shop and Hester both galloping downhill, or so it seemed. I hadn't seen her for nearly three years — I had been in Western Australia. I couldn't get back instantly, either — well, to tell you the truth I didn't realize the urgency. I stayed on to wind up things there.' He sighed deeply and Clare could see this weighed on him.

'But you did get here,' she eventually put

into the silence that now hung between them.

'Yep, I made it at last — and did my best. I stayed with her, of course, and took the shop off her hands. But there wasn't a great deal I could do there — it had become more of a drag than an asset. I had no idea when I first got back that she was as ill as she was. I knew it must be pretty bad or she would never have asked me to come, but I had no idea she actually had such a very short time to live. It was a terrible shock when she died so soon after I got here.' He paused, then added, 'Barely three weeks,' seeming to pick up the question in Clare's mind although she had not spoken it aloud.

'Oh, how dreadful.' It sounded banal and totally inadequate but Clare could find nothing else to say.

'It was.' Mark at least seemed to find her response adequate. 'She just had time to put me in the picture — tell me about you and what her main wishes were.'

Clare digested this. 'About me? But she didn't know anything about me, did she?'

'On the contrary, she knew just about everything about you.'

'How could she? The only time, as far as I know, that we met was that occasion when I was very small.'

'I didn't say she knew you, I said she knew about you.'

'I don't understand — how could she?' Then as another thought struck her, 'If that was so then why didn't I know anything about her?'

Mark didn't answer; instead he downed his tools and abruptly changed the subject. 'We have done about all we can do here today. Tomorrow we will start painting. I don't know about you but I am tired, hungry and very, very dirty.'

'Me, too,' Clare agreed with a sigh, as following his example she too put away her cleaning tools. She looked across the empty room at him, intending to ask more, but his face had a shutdown look and she knew that she would get no more answers at the moment to the questions that bedevilled her. Oh well, there was always another time.

She realized as she followed Mark out and waited while he locked up the shop that she was indeed very, very tired. It had been a long time since she had done such a stint of physical work. But it was a good feeling, quite different to the way she felt after a long day at the office grappling with other people's problems.

Back at the cottage, when Mark let her in, she wondered when he would give her a key to her own front door. 'You can have the shower first,' he told her, 'I'll take Boris for a quick run. He needs the exercise and the fresh air will do me good after working in that dust and dirt.'

Me too, Clare thought to herself, but unwilling to push herself on him and anxious to clean up, she accepted his offer of first shower graciously.

Either he went for a short walk or she took a long shower for she was still in it when she heard him return. Swiftly she grabbed a towel, wrapped it round her and stepped out of the stall, only to discover that all her clothes were still in the bedroom. After a hurried rub down, she wrapped herself up in what was, fortunately, a very large bath sheet and walked into the hallway where she almost collided with Mark wearing nothing but a very colourful pair of boxer shorts.

For a moment they stared at one another in mutual embarrassment, then Clare found her eyes drawn from his face to his naked torso at the same time as she felt the thick towel slip off one shoulder. She raised her eyes back to his face in time to watch his own gaze lift from her bare skin to her face. For what seemed a long time, although in actual fact probably only seconds passed, they stared at one another. Clare felt as if her whole body

271

was flushing beneath the towel and heard her breath catch in a funny little gasp.

'I — I'm sorry — I should have been out. I didn't realize I had taken so long . . . ' she stammered. 'It's all yours now.' She gave an involuntary gesture towards the bathroom and as she did so the towel slipped even further, revealing the soft moulding of her breast. Seeing his gaze slip downward again she snatched at the rough fabric with an embarrassed half-laugh.

Mark's features, to her astonishment, broke into a wide grin. 'We are married, you know,' he reminded her as he stepped past her to the bathroom door. Halfway through he turned back, his grin even wider if possible. 'V-e-r-y nice!' he drawled and disappeared, closing the door behind him with a firm click.

For a few seconds Clare remained where she was, staring at the closed door, feeling rather spaced out, then she went into the bedroom and began to dress. As she stood at the mirror, running a comb through her damp hair, she noticed that her eyes looked unnaturally bright and two spots of colour burned in her cheeks. 'I look drunk!' she said aloud, adding under her breath, 'Or like some starry-eyed teenager in love for the first time.' Well, she was neither. So she gave her hair another vigorous rub with the towel, then had to comb it again, and deftly applied a light make-up, choosing a soft pink lipstick that matched her shirt. Then, with a deep breath, she made her way out to the kitchen to see what she could find to eat. She was as hungry as Mark had said he was.

She was standing in front of the open fridge, assessing its limited contents, when she heard Mark come out of the bathroom. Unlike her, he had remembered to take clothes in with him and was now dressed in a clean pair of jeans and a shirt whose blue material almost matched his eyes.

'I guess it is a bit like Mother Hubbard's cupboard, isn't it?'

'I'm afraid so, but in our cupboard there isn't even a bone for Boris!'

'Not to worry about him — I have plenty of tins. I usually feed him raw meat but I do keep tins for emergencies. But that's probably all there is in the pantry. I don't fancy tinned dog food much, do you? So how about we go out for dinner?'

Clare shut the fridge door and turned to him with an acquiescent nod. 'That sounds like the best idea either of us has had all day.'

'Give me ten minutes to feed Boris and we'll be off.' Mark smiled. It was barely eight minutes later, Clare observed as she checked her watch, they were walking out of the house. They took her car because, as Mark pointed out, they were both now squeaky-clean and his car had collected a good deal of the grime and detritus removed from the shop earlier on.

Clare nodded agreement, wondering if he simply meant what he said or if there was some underlying message there. 'Hell no,' she told herself. 'Don't start looking for hidden meanings in everything — just enjoy yourself!'

And that is exactly what she did, finding a lightheartedness in Mark's company she had not known for a long time. She also realized how little she actually knew about this man who was now her husband, even if in name only, and with the thought came the decision to remedy things on both counts.

'What was it like living in Western Australia?' she asked him as they sat companionably side by side on high stools at the bar enjoying a pre-dinner drink. Adding, when he didn't answer immediately, 'I've never been there, but I believe it is very beautiful.'

'In parts, yes, but it is such a huge state, about half Australia. Wish I had seen more of it now I am back here but you know how it is — you always think there is plenty of time to do everything. Then suddenly there isn't.' He looked pensively into his glass and she had the feeling that he wasn't really thinking about Western Australia's huge terrain. 'I was in Perth — as capital cities go it is a very pleasant place, with a climate that is supposed to be much like that of Cape Town.'

'Oh,' Clare mumbled. As she knew even less about South Africa than she did about Western Australia she was not much wiser. 'Did you like being an accountant?'

'You're joking! I hated it, but I didn't realize quite how much till I stopped doing it.'

'Yes . . . ' Clare said thoughtfully. As he spoke she was beginning to realize how much she disliked her own job.

'Why did you go into it?' she asked. The words were spoken aloud but she felt she was asking them as much of herself as of Mark.

He shrugged. 'I was always good at maths, so it seemed the obvious way to go, and of course it is a well-paid profession. Have you ever met an accountant short of a buck?' He shrugged then laughed self-deprecatingly. 'Of course you haven't — or, I guess, a solicitor?' There was a slight edge to his voice and he gave her a keen look which stung Clare into agreeing.

'Or a solicitor — which is probably why I went into law.' Their eyes met and held for a moment, as if, thought Clare, they were throwing down the gauntlet in some way; maybe challenging each other to admit to having a soft centre buried somewhere.

'I think our table is ready,' Mark said as he placed his empty glass down deliberately on the counter. 'Shall we go in?'

They had a pleasant meal accompanied by conversation that ranged over a great many subjects, none of them personal, and at the end of it, when they finally got up to go, Clare realized that she knew very little more about Mark than she had some hours earlier. She, on the other hand, was far more susceptible than she had believed. Why else should her skin tingle and her heart jump each time he touched her, however accidentally or lightly?

'You drive . . . please.' Clare held out her car keys. 'I — I think I've probably drunk too much to drive.'

'We both probably have,' he replied drily, but he took the keys and moved round to the driver's side as Clare slid into the passenger seat.

It wasn't, Clare thought, alcohol that would make her driving hazardous but the proximity of Mark himself. She felt a warm glow where his left arm touched her right as he settled into the seat and reached for the seat belt. It spread slowly through her body till her entire self felt infused. She closed her eyes briefly and settled back to enjoy the ride and his nearness.

They drove for the most part in silence, but it was a companionable one, not in any way uncomfortable or strained. When they were inside the house, however, it was different; in the harsh electric light they stood and looked at one another. It was Mark who broke the silence. 'How about a cup of tea?' he asked prosaically. Without waiting for an answer he turned away from her into the kitchen and she heard him filling the jug and switching it on. Following him, she opened the fridge and reached for the milk while he collected mugs. It was a homely domestic scene such as might take place between any husband and wife. But they of course were not any husband and wife.

They didn't speak till they were sitting opposite each other with their mugs cradled in their hands.

'It will be good to start on the painting in the morning,' Clare said at last, more to fill the silence hanging between them than anything else.

'It will,' he agreed, somewhat absently. 'You don't have to do this, you know, Clare. I mean, if you don't want to, there is no obligation . . . ' He trailed off, looking uncomfortable.

'Don't you want me to?' she asked in a small voice, made even smaller by the lump in her throat. She looked down into her half-empty mug, painfully aware of the childish pricking behind her lids; in fact she felt in her sudden hurt that she was reduced to a child. She heard his stool being pushed back from the counter. Some part of her mind registered the fact that it had actually been pushed so vigorously it had fallen over. Then she felt his hands on her shoulders and in some way he was turning her round and standing her up at the same time, for she was sure she did not do it of her own volition.

'Of course I want you to help me — you are a great worker.' He grinned as he said this. 'But I have to be fair. We agreed that our marriage was a business arrangement — a means for you to get the house you want and me to get the shop. No ties, no strings attached, and in due course we would go our separate ways ... ' His voice had a gritty tone.

She looked up and as their eyes met she was astonished to hear herself say, 'Is the agreement written in stone? Suppose one of us wants to change all that? What then?'

'Then I guess we ... ' She never heard what they would do — or maybe Mark didn't get around to actually suggesting it. Instead she found herself held tight in the circle of two strong arms as his lips, warm and very demanding, met hers.

As they drew apart, Clare found they were moving in the direction of the main bedroom. He stopped just inside the door and, looking at her quizzically, said, 'Well, Mrs Fisk, have you any objection to getting into honeymoon mode?'

'None at all, Mr Fisk, but I must warn you that I am a modern professional woman and do not believe that women should sacrifice their identity in marriage. I shall remain Clare Davenport!'

He stared at her for a moment, then burst out laughing. 'Fair enough — Clare Davenport!' he said as he picked her up and carried her into the bedroom. 'I believe that is customary, and I am old-fashioned enough to want to do it.' She didn't remind him that it was the threshold he was supposed to carry her over, and he had already done that; she was finding the experience altogether too enjoyable. Independence was one thing, but in the face of such masterful masculinity it tended to wilt.

His movements were slow, deliberate, devoid of the frenzied ripping off of garments that she had grown accustomed to with Robert. It had been flattering at first, especially as in most things he did he was anything but reckless or hasty; the implication that he couldn't get enough of her and couldn't get it fast enough. Latterly it had palled somewhat and she had got into the habit of taking her own clothes off the minute they were alone together. With Mark everything seemed, by comparison, to be in slow motion and she found herself responding to him, like a flower opening to the sun.

As they lay together, both of them naked, she looked deep into his eyes and had the sensation of falling, almost drowning, in their depths. 'Mark?' she breathed his name softly, on a rising inflection making a question of it, although she wasn't sure what she was asking. Then her vision blurred as his face came closer, she shut her eyes and gave herself up to the sensation of their bodies cleaving together; with a muffled gasp she locked her legs round him and arched to meet him.

Later, when they lay together in the dreamy surcease that is the normal aftermath of good love-making, she ran her finger slowly down his arm, absently smoothing the hairs as she went, and asked, 'Where did you learn to make love so beautifully?' She hadn't really intended to compliment him by asking a question, this was just the way it came out. She was surprised to feel tension in the limb beneath her caressing finger, and it was echoed somehow in his voice when he finally replied, 'The same way as you, I guess.'

Her question had been mere idle musing, but his answer hit her with a ping, almost as if he had spat a paper pellet at her from a pea-shooter. Even as she felt like this, she recognized she was being totally unreasonable. 'But I thought — ' She began, then stopped abruptly, remembering that whatever lay in his past was his.

'It was over — long ago.'

'Oh, I — I'm sorry. What happened?' She hadn't meant to probe; the question seemed to slip out of its own volition.

'She . . . died,' he said tonelessly, just when she thought he wasn't going to answer at all.

'Oh.' Sensing he had withdrawn from her in some indefinable way, she moved closer to him physically as if to counteract it.

Mark turned to face her, as he did so pushing away slightly so that he could look into her face. 'What about you? Your liaison with Robert, is it really over, Clare?'

She stiffened in his arms, hurt that he apparently doubted her. 'Of course. I told you it was. You believe me?'

He sighed. 'Yes, I believe you. That was quite unforgivable of me. It's just that, well, sometimes the past seems to come back to spoil the future.'

'I don't think I know what you mean.'

'No, I don't suppose you do.' He sighed. 'I'll explain it all to you one day. For now tell me what it was about Robert that made your relationship last two years, and why you decided to end it.'

'It was really good, in the beginning . . . ' she began hesitantly. 'I suppose I was in love with him, yes, of course I was — it wasn't just that I was flattered.'

'Why were you flattered? Is he so special?' He didn't wait for an answer but went on to say, 'Surely you must have had dozens of people in love you? After all you are a very attractive person.'

Clare shook her head. 'No, he was the first who seemed to fall in love with me.'

'Come on now — I simply can't believe that!'

'Well, it's true. I — I didn't go out much. Even at college I kept my nose to the grindstone. I knew I had to do well if I didn't want to fall into the same sort of rut that my parents had. Anyway, Dad didn't really like me going out, not with boys anyway, then he fell sick and I couldn't . . . Well, it was difficult. There was no one but me to look after him.'

As Mark listened he realized that her much vaunted independence was a mere façade, or sort of skin she had grown to protect herself.

Clare wondered for a moment if he thought her naïve — worse, stupid. The fleeting fear vanished as he drew her closer to his body. As the physical desire that had awakened between them flared again in a sharp burst, Clare offered him her body with an abandonment she had seldom, if ever, shown to Robert.

She woke next morning to find the half of the bed that Mark had occupied empty. She rolled over and looked at the bedside clock — it was barely 6.30, but he had probably got up to take that monster hound for a walk. Goodness knows, with legs like he had, the creature needed plenty of exercise. She pulled the bedclothes back up round her chin and decided to stay where she was, but she didn't drop off to sleep. She found that her mind had gone into overdrive and she was thinking about Mark in much the same way that she thought about her clients when she was working out how to best untangle them and get the best deal in the process. Something nibbled round her thoughts, something that was not quite right. What had he said, something about marriage, she couldn't remember whether he had actually said it, or just implied it, but she was sure he had suggested at least that he had been married before. This she was sure could not be true, for there was nothing at all about a previous marriage in their application to be married.

Irked that he had apparently been less than truthful with her while at the same time coercing her into giving him her entire life story — well, almost — she decided she could not lie there any longer ruminating. She threw back the sheet and was out of bed in a flash, heading for the bathroom with an armful of clothes somewhat indiscriminately snatched up. The house was filled with the peculiar silence of emptiness. From the bathroom window she could see the back yard and there was no sign of Boris. She stepped into the shower stall and turned the taps on full blast, gasping as the first jets pinged on her bare skin with an icy chill.

As she rubbed shampoo into her scalp, relishing the feel of her crisply massaging fingers, she began to hum the catchy 'I'm going to wash that man right out of my hair' from *South Pacific*. She paused briefly to wonder what it was about having a shower that made even the most unmusical burst into song and then again to ask herself just which man she wanted to wash out of her hair — and her life. Until her wandering early morning thoughts, she would have said, quite unhesitatingly, Robert. Now, having come to the conclusion that Mark was not being entirely up front with her, she was not so sure. As she hummed she pluralized the word and sung aloud 'Going to wash those men right out of my hair . . . ' but even as the words joined with the sound of splashing water to float away with the steam she remembered that she had married one of them.

With this sobering thought she closed her mouth, turned off the taps and reached for her towel. When she finally emerged, clean, clear-eyed and — she hoped — clear-headed, it was to the welcome smell of coffee and toast and the sight of Mark looking very domestic in the kitchen.

They spent the next two days steadily painting. They worked for the most part in a companionable near silence, conversation restricted to the work they were doing. At the end of each day they went back to the cottage, tired but satisfied with what they had achieved, cleaned up, ate and went to bed — together. They had settled, it seemed, into a comfortable routine. At the end of the third day, when all the paining was done, Clare looked at the floor, bleak grey concrete. Serviceable enough in a florist's shop but undeniably prosaic, it made a dismal contrast to the bright walls.

'I'm coming back tonight to do that.'

'Tonight!' Clare tried to keep the dismay out of her voice. 'But . . . ' She faltered, not quite brazen enough to say what she was thinking. 'How long will it take you?' she asked.

'A few hours at least — but if I do it tonight that gives it a chance to dry and by tomorrow night, or the day after tomorrow, we should be able to get stock in.'

'Yes.' It made sense. 'What colour are you going to paint it?'

'Oh, I'm not — at least not just one colour. I thought I told you, I'm doing a flower design on it. I thought a gigantic posy.'

Clare thought it sounded pretty ambitious and treacherously wondered if he had the artistic skill to carry it out.

'I'll draw out a rough diagram before we go back,' he told her. 'Can you remember where I put that jar of coloured chalks?'

Clare could — and fetched it for him. She stood back and watched in some admiration as he drew on the grey cement a gigantic bunch of flowers in the centre of the floor. When he had done, they both stepped back and looked at it: even though he had only done the outlines of the leaves and flowers it was impressive.

'Mark!' she exclaimed. 'That's really wonderful!'

'It will look a good deal better when I have painted it in.' His tone was modest but he looked pleased by her praise. 'Come on now — let's go home and have something to eat then I will get back here and do it.'

Clare cooked omelettes while Mark made salad for a quick meal. 'No wine — not till I get back anyway,' Mark told her. 'I need a steady hand for this job. And no,' he added, 'I would rather you did not come. I don't want distractions either.'

As she watched him leave, Clare wasn't sure whether or not she liked being classified as a distraction. Left alone, she washed up their few dishes then showered. She had just returned to the lounge-room, hair still damp, when Boris announcing there was someone on the premises shattered the silence. The doorbell was almost drowned in his vociferous voice. She heard a male voice speaking to him and silence returned.

'Timothy!' Clare exclaimed. 'Nice to see you — come in.' She wasn't being strictly truthful. 'Mark is up at the shop, painting. He — '

'I know,' Timothy interrupted. 'I saw him. 'It's you I really want to see.'

'Oh?' Clare wondered what it was about

him that made her feel she had done something wrong or, even more subtly, failed to do the right thing. 'Come in — sit down. What would you like? tea, coffee or something stronger?'

'I think maybe . . . ' He hesitated before saying in a rush, 'You wouldn't have any whisky, would you?'

'I — I'm not sure.' Clare went to the cupboard where she knew Mark kept drinks and was glad to see a whisky bottle almost two-thirds full. 'Yes, we have. How would you like it?'

'Just a dash of water and a small amount of ice.' Clare poured it, then impulsively got a second glass for herself. If Timothy needed Dutch courage to tell her whatever it was he had come to tell her, then she probably did too in order to hear it.

She passed him his glass and sat down opposite him. Timothy swirled the liquid round as he gazed into his glass. Clare found she was doing the same and for a moment the only sound in the room was the clink of ice against glass. Clare was the first to raise her glass to her lips. Looking directly at him, she raised her eyebrows and murmured, 'Well, Timothy, what have you come to tell me?'

Timothy gave another swirl then took a long sip before saying, 'I have had a phone call from your . . . er . . . friend Robert.'

'From Robert? Clare was astonished. 'But why on earth would he — '

'About the will.'

'Ah yes!' Clare remembered he had said something about contacting Timothy to sort it out, but that was before they'd split up. 'He did say ... but that was ages ago ... Before ... ' At this point she stalled, hopelessly. 'Does it matter now? After all, Mark and I are married. Surely it's all sorted out. Boris is here in his own home as you saw when you arrived, Mark is in his shop, happy as a sandboy, and I'm here for the moment.'

'In your dream cottage.'

'Yes.' Clare took another gulp of her whisky, gasping slightly as it hit her throat, and glared somewhat defiantly at Timothy. 'What is wrong with all that?'

He looked down into his glass, then looking up, said slowly, 'He seems to think the whole thing is rather irregular — that you were coerced into marriage. He has accused me of misrepresenting the will to you to get things going the way you wanted.' He suddenly looked sharply at Clare. 'I have to admit he is a rather better lawyer than you or me. Didn't you think the will was odd, to say the least? You didn't seem to question it much. Or I guess even read what I gave you very well.'

Clare was an astute enough lawyer to pick up on the last words. 'What do you mean, what you gave me? Are you telling me that you only gave me part of the will? Can you explain just what you mean?' she asked coolly, adopting her legal voice.

Timothy shuffled on his seat and didn't seem as if he wanted to meet her eyes. When he did speak it seemed totally irrelevant to Clare.

'Mark and I go back a long way — we have been friends for many years.'

He paused at this point and Clare interrupted with some acidity. 'Which of course is why you were at our wedding.' Timothy looked even more uncomfortable and she added, 'Or was there another reason?'

'We both knew your Aunt Hester very well indeed, and in a way we knew you too.'

'None of you, Mark, Hester and certainly not you, knew me at all. The first time I met you was when I came to see you in your office.'

'I said I, we, knew you 'in a way'. I should probably have said we knew about you.' He paused again and Clare waited. Finally he added, 'Your aunt had very strict, you might say old-fashioned, notions about things.'

'What on earth has that got to do with anything?'

'She didn't like the idea of you having a relationship with someone who was married.'

Clare gaped at him. 'But she didn't know me. The last time she met me I was only a little girl. I can barely remember meeting her.'

'She remembered that meeting very well indeed.'

'Maybe she did but ... ' Clare was beginning to feel out of her depth.

'Your father should have contacted her after your mother died. Why didn't he?'

Clare shrugged. 'I don't know. Maybe if she was so strait-laced he didn't want her to know that his marriage was such a disaster.' She gave another small shrug. 'Look, I just don't know. He didn't confide in me that much. I think at times he rather regretted taking me on. I have no doubt he found me a bit of a drag, to say the least. Sometimes I wished he hadn't too.' She stopped suddenly and stared at Timothy as if she had only just realized he was there. 'God knows why I am telling you all this.'

It was his turn to shrug now, somewhat dismissively, as if he had found listening to her rather a drag, Clare thought. 'We — I knew most of it anyway.'

'What do you mean 'we'? Are you talking about my aunt, someone else or indulging in the royal we?'

291

'Oh, your aunt and us.'

'Us being?'

'Mark and I, of course.'

'Mark!' Timothy's casual mention of his name hit her like a douche of cold water. 'Are you telling me that Mark was in on this, whatever it is? I think, Timothy, that you owe me an explanation.'

'Certainly. If you can listen calmly without getting all high and mighty and uptight.'

'I'll try. But please keep it simple.'

'Well . . . ' Timothy finally sighed after a silence so lengthy that Clare wondered if it would ever be broken. With an effort she remained quiet and mentally willed him to continue. 'Well,' he repeated, 'you are your Aunt Hester's only living blood relation — '

'I know that,' Clare could not stop herself snapping. Timothy looked pained but otherwise ignored her interruption.

'That being so, she was most anxious that you should be her heir.'

Clare nodded to encourage him to keep talking. For some reason he seemed to be finding it difficult to find the right words.

'But the problem was she didn't know you. She had seen you once as a small child. Then your mother took you to England. She didn't know till fairly recently that your father had brought you back again.' Timothy looked up at her and leaned forward on his elbows. 'Why in the name of all that's holy didn't he come and see the old girl? He was her nephew, after all.'

'I don't know.' Clare shrugged. 'He never even mentioned her to me. That one visit was all I knew of her. I would like to have known her; we had no one here, Dad and I. There was just the two of us, and that was it. It was pretty hard when he got sick and died.' Her lips twisted as she remembered those dreadful days. It would have been good then to have had someone of her own, even an elderly great aunt. She hadn't realized what loneliness was till her father's funeral, when there had been no family at all.

Timothy felt for her; one of a large family himself, he couldn't begin to imagine such total aloneness.

'When did she find out I was here in Australia?'

'Not till some time after your father died. When she knew she was going to die herself actually. By that time you were involved with Robert.'

Clare jumped up and paced the room. She had to move — do something to relieve the choked up feeling that had taken over. Why on earth did her father have to be so stupid? How different her growing up might have been if she had known there was this haven she could escape to. Another thought struck her and she wheeled round on Timothy.

'How did she find out . . . finally?' she demanded. Timothy looked uncomfortable. 'Well?' Clare had no intention of letting him slide out of this one. Suddenly it had become of vital importance to her.

He paused so long that Clare began to wonder if he intended to answer. 'She asked Mark and I to, well, find out about you.' He seemed to have difficulty meeting her gaze.

'And you did? Both of you?'

Timothy nodded.

'Are you telling me that all the time, since, well, since before I even turned up in your office, you and Mark have known all about me?' If Timothy had known her a little better he would have recognized the quiet tone of her voice as the calm before the storm.

He nodded. 'Well yes, I suppose you could say that.'

'I guess you could! And Mark and I — this marriage — ' She spat out the word. 'Was that organized ages ago, all part of the master plan or something?'

Timothy mumbled again.

'Well?' Clare demanded, before, unable to keep her cool, she hurled a cushion at him.

'Go home! Just go!' With a supreme effort

she kept her voice something just below a screech.

He opened his mouth to reply, thought better of it and snapping it shut hurried out of the room. A few seconds later Clare heard the outer door close. She sat quite still for a moment, staring into space with a bleak lost look, then pulled herself together with a visible and obvious effort and headed for the room she had shared so recently and so happily with Mark. Then she remembered that most of her stuff was still in the spare bedroom.

Frantically she stuffed her clothes into her case with scant regard for how they would look on arrival; the important thing was to get them in. At first she thought of just leaving, then the temptation to write a cutting and pithy note was too strong. Unfortunately when she located a sheet of paper and a pen she couldn't think of anything to say that would express her feelings. Finally she scrawled on the paper: *'Ask yourself why I'm not here — and if you don't have the answer try your friend Timothy.'* She placed it face up on the bench then looked round for something solid to put on top of it. A hunk of rose quartz crystal stood on the window sill over the sink. She had admired it before. Holding it in her hand, she looked now into its blushing opaque depths and as she turned it round the light made a small interior rainbow glow catch her eye. 'Just a flaw in the crystal,' she told herself, and yet that small glow of colour in some odd way made her heart lift so that as she placed it on top of the scrap of paper and turned to go, a shard of hope pierced her interior gloom.

13

Clare walked out of the house and closed the door behind her without looking back. She hurried to her car hoping that Mark would not come home before she got away and stop her. At least, she told herself that was what she hoped and firmly repressed the small voice that said the opposite.

Once away from the cottage, she pointed the bonnet of her car towards the highway to Melbourne and just drove. The radio came on as she started, some love song which she mentally categorized as 'slush', and hastily switched over to the CD she had in the player. This was worse, it was Josh Grocan, whose voice alone was enough to melt her bones, singing 'You Raise Me Up'. She had purchased the CD to get this particular song; now she couldn't bear to hear it and flicked back to the radio, fiddling with her left hand to change channels. When she got some incredibly dreary and utterly depressing political talk she decided that this suited her present mood and turned the sound up slightly in a fit of masochism. Her thoughts, however, were louder than any radio could ever be.

She forced herself to concentrate on the road ahead, telling herself that the perfidy of two stupid men was not sufficient reason to play Russian roulette with her own life. She would just return to Melbourne, her flat and her job, and continue with her life as if nothing had happened. But of course it had — she had got married. Ah, well, she comforted herself, that was never meant to be a permanent state anyway. The only problem was that with a sharp stab she realized that whatever had been meant, that wasn't what she wanted. She wished with all her heart that she had learned all this before she realized just how much Mark had taken over her thoughts and feelings. 'Damn him!' she said aloud. 'Damn him to hell!'

She felt marginally better after this outburst, but did not trust her unstable emotions enough to risk returning to the CD.

By the time she drove into the suburbs of Melbourne it was well into the night. She felt very tired, and rather foolish, even to the point of asking herself whether it would not have been better to have stayed and confronted Mark with her new-found knowledge and demanded an explanation. Maybe he had one — although she could not imagine it would be acceptable to her.

The flat, once her haven, felt anything but welcoming as she slid her key into the lock and pushed open the door to grope for the light switch. The comfort from the light was marginal as it revealed the bleak emptiness of the place. No friendly clutter as she had tidied very thoroughly the night before her wedding. The only sign of life was the green light blinking on her answering service.

She walked across and pressed the play button, more out of habit than because she had any desire to get the message. The voice that came through sounded both urgent and angry; it was also familiar. What on earth was Robert doing telephoning her now — when it was far too late for anything?

'Clare! Clare!' he called out. 'Pick up if you are there, please. I must talk to you. It is very important. Are you there?' he repeated. She heard him sigh audibly before he added, 'Ring me back, then, as soon as you get this message — it is of the utmost urgency.' The message ended and she waited for the disembodied voice to tell her the date and time of the call. It was about two minutes after she left the flat the previous Saturday to marry Mark.

There were three more messages after that one, two of them from Robert urging her to contact him 'before it is too late'. Clare shrugged and smiled ruefully to herself; if he meant by that before she married Mark then she was too late, if he meant while there was still hope of reviving their relationship then he was too late. The third message was some unknown voice apologizing for getting the wrong number.

Clare systematically wiped each message, then went through to the bedroom where she threw herself down on the bed and, in spite of the thoughts whirling through her head, went out like a light. Her last conscious thought was to wonder what the hell Robert wanted.

She woke to the sound of thunderous knocking on her door interspersed with the ringing of the doorbell. 'All right, I'm coming,' she muttered as she swung her legs over the edge of the bed, wondering as she did so why Boris wasn't barking. Her feet had hit the floor before she realized that it was because he was not there.

A glance at her watch told her that she had only been asleep for a couple of hours and it was still the early hours of the morning. Pulling her clothes closer round her body, she opened the door cautiously.

'Robert! What on earth are you doing here at this hour?' she demanded. 'How did you know I was here? I didn't — '

'No, you didn't return my calls. Why not? I

tried to make it clear to you how urgent it was.'

'I didn't get them till a short while ago,' Clare grumbled, bemused by sleep. 'I've only just got back. How did you know I was back anyway?' she demanded.

'I tried to get you again — on impulse — and the phone rang through, so I knew you must be back if you had switched your answerphone off.'

'Oh,' Clare said weakly, adding, 'I didn't hear the phone ring.'

'Well, it did. But not for long — as soon as I realized you were home I got in the car and came round here. I saw your car so knew you were back, from wherever. You took some rousing!'

'I was tired, still am,' Clare told him, moving back into the flat as she spoke. 'Well, I suppose as you are here and I am now awake, if not thoroughly, you'd better come in.' Grudgingly she moved back from the door to let him pass before closing it again, yawning as she did so and running her hands through her hair. 'God, Robert this better be good — I'm bushed.'

'Oh, it's good all right. Maybe good isn't quite the word. Important, I should say.' He looked round hopefully. 'Got any coffee?'

'No. You woke me up. However,' she added after a brief pause in which she recognized

301

that she was in desperate need of something to get herself going, at least to rouse her sufficiently to cope with Robert and whatever it was he had to say, 'I'll make some.' Uncomfortably aware that she was still in the clothes she had driven home in, she felt very much at a disadvantage. She ran her fingers in a combing gesture through her hair in a somewhat futile effort to tidy it as she plugged in the electric jug and spooned coffee into the plunger. As she waited for the water to boil she laid out mugs, milk and sugar and then rubbed at her eyes with clenched fists in a childish gesture that made her appear both young and vulnerable. If Robert had been in the mood to be touched, it must surely have affected him.

Clare kept her back to him as she poured the boiling water into the coffee plunger and placed it on the kitchen bench. She did not have sufficient faith in her ability to stay awake if she took it to the lounge and allowed herself to drop into an easy chair. Nor did she want to be too welcoming to Robert.

She pressed down the plunger and poured coffee for them both pushing one of the mugs across the bench to Robert. 'Well?'

He poured milk into his coffee, added sugar and stirred it thoughtfully. 'I have been doing some research, looking into things,' he said at last.

'You too?' Clare muttered, half under her breath. If he heard, he ignored the comment.

'I can't think why you didn't do it yourself. After all you are a lawyer. I can't believe you just accepted what this Timothy Whatsit told you.'

'Trimble, Timothy Trimble,' Clare interjected. Somehow she wanted to stop Robert from making any damaging disclosures — she felt she had heard more than enough.

'What? Yes, Trimble. Do stop interrupting me, Clare. Anyway, I got hold of a copy of the will and — '

'Damn the bloody will!' Clare exploded. Suddenly she had heard more than enough. She never wanted to hear the word will again. It had disrupted her whole life.

'I would appreciate it if you could just keep quiet and listen to me.' How pompous he sounded. 'As I was saying, I got hold of a copy of the will and it seems you could stand to gain a great deal. In fact, you would be quite a wealthy woman. All you had to do was agree to giving that dog a home — and after all, that need be no big drama, dogs can get lost, have accidents, die of natural causes. If you — we — just agreed to take it . . . I will

303

soon be free and we could get married like we always planned.'

'Are you suggesting, Robert, that I should take B — I mean, the dog on and then dispose of him?' Forgetting that she had been quite appalled in the first place at the idea of taking that giant canine under her wing, Clare felt a sudden rush of affection for him, and with it one of revulsion for Robert. 'That hardly seems quite, well, ethical to me.' She had momentarily missed the significance of Robert's remark about getting married.

Robert shrugged. 'Ethics?' He sounded genuinely surprised. 'Where do they come into it? After all, it's only an old dog we are talking about here. I expect you could find him another home if it really bothered you. But you could hardly turn down your entire inheritance for him.'

Clare was opening her mouth to say that not only could she but she had when there was a thunderous knock on the door followed by the bell ringing as if someone had their finger stuck to it.

'What the hell?' Robert exploded, adding, 'Don't open it — you don't know who — '

But Clare was already there, drawing back the bolt, wondering in some part of her mind why she had used it in the first place. Surely she hadn't wanted to keep Robert in?

'Clare, are you all right?' Mark, obviously reassured to see her standing in front of him, didn't wait for an answer but pushed past her into the flat.

'What are you doing here?' he demanded of Robert in a dangerously quiet voice.

'What the hell are you doing?' Robert retorted.

'I've come to collect Clare.' Mark's tone was steely and his eyes matched his voice as he looked at Robert.

'I don't think so. Clare and I will be getting married very shortly, won't we, darling?' He turned to Clare as he spoke. Something in her expression must have alerted him to the fact that things were not exactly all going his way for his voice faltered and finally tailed off. He looked from one to the other, for the first time since he had arrived showing signs of uncertainty.

'I think not, mate.' Mark managed to make the common Australian word used between men as a sign of friendliness sound anything but. 'You're a bit late — Clare and I were married last weekend. I've come to make sure my wife is not being molested — in any way, physically or verbally.' He turned to Clare. 'Has he touched you?' he demanded.

She shook her head, then turned back to Robert. 'I'm sorry, Robert, really I am — I just didn't realize you didn't know. I haven't seen you for a few weeks and I suppose it was rather quick — and we did have a very quiet wedding.' She stopped, wondering why she was gabbling like this, apologizing, almost grovelling. She moved to the door. 'I think perhaps you had better go.'

Robert moved to the door in sharp jerky movements. 'I most certainly will. But,' he added vehemently, 'don't think you have heard the last of this — either of you.'

'What does he mean?' Clare asked as the door slammed behind him. 'There is nothing he can do, is there?'

Suddenly everything seemed overwhelming; she felt as if she were in some nightmare and wondered what on earth she had done to deserve such a mess. It seemed that every man she spoke to in the last few hours had it in for her in some way. She looked at Mark, painfully aware that the sudden trembling in her limbs was in danger of reaching her mouth. 'I don't know what you are really here for — but after what I have learned tonight I don't see any point in you staying either.'

'I thought I had made it clear why I was here. I have come to find you.'

'Well, I can't say I particularly like being followed half way across Australia any more than I like being got out of bed and haranced by Robert.'

Mark grinned. 'Have you looked at a map of Australia lately? A couple of hours driving in Victoria is hardly 'half way' across Australia!'

'Oh, don't be so — so bloody pedantic! You know perfectly well what I mean. I don't like being followed, chased up, checked on by anyone.'

'It seems to me it is quite a good job I did follow you. If I hadn't, Bluebeard there might have carted you off to add to his harem.'

'Now you are being ridiculous.'

'Am I, Clare? I don't think so. If you want to go with him I am not stopping you; but you can't run from everyone for ever, you know.' Mark looked at the coffee mugs and plunger on the bench. 'Do you think I could have a cup of coffee?' he asked humbly.

Clare moved silently over and refilled the jug. 'This is pretty cold now,' she said prosaically. 'I'll make another pot.' She ran her hand wearily through her hair. 'I guess we both could do with it.'

'Were you going some place?'

'No.' Clare wondered why he asked; then realized that she was still wearing the clothes she had left Maldon in the day before. She gave a somewhat weak and wobbly smile. 'I was so exhausted I dropped to sleep like this last night,' she admitted, her nose wrinkled in self-disgust. 'I guess I must look, and smell, pretty frightful. I'd better go and shower.' The electric jug came to the boil and switched itself off.

'Not so fast,' Mark admonished, forestalling her by getting up quickly and pouring the water on the fresh coffee Clare had already put in the plunger. 'Have a cuppa with me first. I don't mind how you look — or smell,' he added as he collected a fresh mug for himself and put the refilled plunger down between them.

Clare half expected him to add, 'I'm used to it.' But if he thought it he refrained from saying anything. Instead he asked, with no banter in his voice, only what sounded, even to her, as if he cared, 'Whatever made you do it, Clare?'

'Do what? Marry you? A moment of temporary insanity, I think.'

'Don't be like that. I want to know — I care.' For the second time Clare thought he really sounded as if he did. She concentrated on pushing the plunger down, afraid that if she looked up in her present weakened state she would probably burst into tears.

'I've told you — temporary insanity.' She poured him coffee and pushed the mug towards him, hesitated for a moment then refilled her own. At this moment death by caffeine poisoning sounded a reasonable option.

They sipped hot coffee in silence for a few minutes then Mark repeated slowly, and carefully, as if he was talking to someone who had difficulty understanding simple English. 'Please, Clare, I need to know. Why on earth did you take off like that? Everything was hunky dory between us — at least I thought it was, when I left you to finish that painting. I came back, full of the satisfaction of a job well done, and found you gone. I asked Boris what had happened, but he wasn't much help . . . ' Here Clare could not help a small wobbly giggle; she bit her lip and screwed up her eyes in a childish attempt to stop the traitorous tears spilling over. 'So when he had told me nothing and I had searched in every conceivable part of the cottage, I finally had the wit to go and see if your car was outside.'

'I should have thought the fact that it wasn't would have been obvious when you got home,' Clare interrupted somewhat caustically.

'Well, it wasn't. I suppose my mind was on what I had just been doing and looking forward to seeing you again — talking to you, telling you things, making plans.'

'Oh, that all sounds so nice, so very nice.

But how do you expect me to swallow one word of it after — after — ' Clare gulped past the lump in her throat and struggled on. 'After Timothy came and explained things to me.'

'What do you mean, Timothy explained things to you? Just what did he tell you?' It seemed to Clare that his voice was sharp with concern that Timothy had told her things he didn't want her to know; 'spilled the beans' in some way.

She got up with a sigh of pure weariness, physical and emotional. 'I'm going to have a shower,' she told him. 'You don't have to worry — I withdraw all claim to my Aunt Hester's estate. I suppose she *was* really that — my aunt I mean. It seems to me you and Timothy probably have more claim than I do, deserve it more, anyway. I never knew her, never did a thing for her, never knew about the house, the shop, Boris, anything. What you don't have, or know about, you don't miss — or so they say.' She studiously kept her eyes off Mark's face as she attempted to go past him to the door and the bathroom. But when he jumped to his feet, blocked her way and grabbed her by both arms, just above the elbow, she was left with little choice but to look directly into his face.

Not for long, though. With a superhuman

effort she pulled her gaze back from those see-all blue eyes and looked down, and so missed the change of expression as they darkened in sudden anger. When he shook her, none too gently, it came as a shock.

'You are the most exasperating person I have ever known,' he told her. 'Worse than that, you are so stupid I don't know why on earth I bother with you!'

This unexpected outburst ignited a spark of anger in Clare and, struggling to free her arms while still exercising sufficient self-control not to look into his face, she spat back, 'Don't then! I certainly don't want you to. You're a bossy, domineering, self-righteous' — here she ran short of adjectives — 'person who has no right, no right at all to go poking about in other people's lives . . . and . . . and I hate you!' The last bit came out in a wobbly tremble that sounded like a two-year-old in the throes of a temper tantrum. In that moment she hated herself even more and was taken completely unawares when he not only loosened her arms but seemed to thrust her away from him so that she staggered backwards into a kitchen stool and finally on to the floor.

At this point she gave up and burst into tears. For a moment Mark just stared at her as if he couldn't believe he had really done that, then gabbling wild and profuse apologies he stepped forward, grabbed her hand and pulled her to her feet and into his arms. Clare, feeling drained of her last bit of physical strength and will power and afraid her legs were about to stop supporting her, leaned weakly against his chest and let the tears flow.

As she sobbed, rather noisily and very damply, against Mark's chest, she felt she had gone beyond exhaustion, almost beyond speech. While part of her felt that she had hit the depths of misery and humiliation, another part of herself was relishing the comfort and borrowed strength of Mark's arms around her. It was as if she had reached a haven that she never wanted to leave.

His voice reminded her, however, that was not possible. She felt, rather than saw, his head drop so that his lips just touched her hair. 'You are absolutely bushed,' he told her. 'Go shower and sleep, or sleep and shower, whatever — do them both. Then when you feel revived we will talk. I'll still be here,' he told her, sensing her sudden fear that he would not. 'Go on now — we need to talk but not till you're in a more fit state.' So gently she scarcely realized what he was doing, he disentangled himself from her and turned her in the direction of the bathroom and bedroom.

Moving like a zombie, Clare went to the

bedroom, peeled off her clothes and slid naked between the sheets. She bad barely hit the pillow before she was asleep.

When she surfaced over two hours later and crossed the hallway to the shower, she was glad she had done it this way round. The warm water was both rousing and soothing at the same time. She rubbed shampoo into her rumpled hair and felt her fingers massaging her scalp, at the same time feeling intense sensual pleasure in the remarkable therapeutic effect of running water, especially warm water sliding off her body in steamy, scented rivulets.

By the time she emerged she was ready, she thought, to talk to Mark and prepared for anything he had to say. She was also very hungry. The smell of coffee hung in the air, probably the last lot they drank, Clare thought, but going into the tiny kitchen saw that Mark was just making a fresh pot.

'You seem a bit short on provisions,' he remarked, 'so I went out and foraged while you were asleep. How does bacon and eggs sound?'

'Heavenly!' Clare was already beginning to drool at the prospect.

'Coming up shortly — very shortly,' Mark promised, turning up the gas jet under the pan he already had sitting there.

'Suppose you tell me what this is all about.' His tone was avuncular as they sat opposite each other to eat.

'No, Mark, suppose you do,' Clare responded, 'I did leave you a note, after all. It's up to you now to give me some sort of explanation.'

He was so long replying that Clare wondered if he was going to. 'I thought Timothy explained it all to you,' he said at last.

'Well, no, he didn't, or yes, he did — or at least he attempted some sort of whitewash of what I feel was totally reprehensible behaviour in what I had assumed was a responsible member of my profession.' Clare realized that not only was she running out of the right words but she was beginning to sound incredibly self-important. Truth to tell so much of her attention was on the plate of bacon and eggs, two, sunny side up, that Mark had just put in front of her that it was hard to put her mind on anything else.

'Thanks — that looks good!' she said in her normal voice, glancing up to smile into his face. When he smiled back she reminded herself quickly that she was delivering a justified complaint to this man and hastily looked down at her plate.

'I should have thought my note was self-explanatory.'

He didn't answer and she was compelled to look up again and meet his amused gaze.

'Oh yes — quite,' he agreed in a mock serious voice, 'but that still doesn't explain what annoyed you so much.'

'Well, I should have thought it was obvious. I don't like to think that I was being checked out like a common criminal.'

'Haven't you ever checked anyone's credentials?'

'No. Well, yes, of course I have but — '

'But it's different when it's you being checked.'

Clare concentrated on her bacon and eggs. She had an uncomfortable feeling that she was not coming out well in this discussion. 'Well, it upset me.' She wished she hadn't said that, it sounded so petulant. Mark ignored it. 'What I want to know is why she, Hester, didn't just contact me, look me over herself, decide for herself whether or not I was a fit heir, not ask you two to do it for her.'

'She was, well, I suppose you would say very strait-laced. According to today's thinking she was. But she didn't like the idea of you living with a married man.'

'I'm not — I didn't. I mean, I never lived with him as in cohabiting,' Clare protested.

'How did she know about our relationship, anyway?' It crossed her mind that if this old aunt of hers had known then it was a cert that Robert's wife had.

Mark shrugged. 'She knew. That's all that matters. But she felt that you had such an unfortunate childhood that it was no wonder. She thought your mother was a gold-digger and was sorry for your father but thought he was weak. She hoped he would contact her when he came back to Australia with you. She was bitterly disappointed and very hurt when he didn't but too proud to contact him. I gather there was some sort of a row between them before he left Australia.'

Clare felt a sadness that suddenly threatened to choke her as she thought of the wasted years — how wonderful it would have been to have had this cottage to visit, a real live aunt of her own, all lost because of the stupid pride of two stubborn people.

'Well, how do you fit in? Explain that to me,' she demanded, sounding angry and harsh even to her own ears.

Mark fiddled with the cutlery on the table. 'It's a long story,' he said at last.

'We've got time. The rest of our lives — if we decide to stay married,' Clare retorted in a dry voice.

'I've told you how I grew up there. My

mother was Hester's companion, house-keeper, closest friend. I grew up in the house and I loved the old girl. But like most young people, when I hit my late teens I was all for getting away, living my own life, finding out about the real world, whatever that is. So I went — about as far as I could — off to Western Australia. Then I met Belinda.' He stopped speaking suddenly and Clare watched an expression of such sadness cross his face that she caught her breath.

After a very long pause she said softly, 'Who was Belinda?' wondering, even as she spoke, if she really wanted to know.

'We were engaged. Hester and Mum wanted me to come over and marry here. I refused; I wanted them to come over there. They refused. I didn't know at the time that my mother was far too ill to even contemplate the journey. She died before our wedding. Maybe it was as well; she never knew what happened.'

'You can't have been married. There was nothing on the application to marry about you being married before.' Clare seized on what to her suddenly seemed of vital importance.

'No, we weren't. Nearly but not quite.' He spoke quietly and slowly as if it was an effort to drag each word out.

In the ensuing silence, Clare had the feeling that he was repeating this story out loud more for his own benefit than for hers, as if in some way he had to make it real before he could wipe the slate clean.

'What happened?' she finally asked in a whisper when she could bear the suspense no longer.

'Belinda was killed two days before our wedding. I was driving.'

'Oh my God!' Clare clapped her hand over her mouth as the horror of this hit and overcame her.

'Were you ... were you hurt?' she whispered at last.

'Not really. Concussion and a broken arm, that was all. I wished at the time that I had been killed too. No, not too, instead of her. I went to pieces when I came out of hospital, hated everyone and everything, myself most of all. I gave up my job and took off out of Perth. For the next six months I just wandered, doing any work I could get, building a hard shell round myself. I wanted to be sure I was never hurt like that again.'

14

Clare felt overcome with a wave of compassion. She could feel the tears stinging her eyes and a lump in her throat, yet mixed with the compassion for Mark was what she felt was a totally selfish concern for herself; she was ashamed of it, but it was there. He had spoken of the protective shield he had painstakingly built round himself, there seemed little chance that she would ever break it down. Like a dying man seeing his life flash before him, she relived the times that she had railed at him and blamed him for things. There was no way he would ever want her. Was that what he was trying to tell her in as gentle a way as possible? She yearned to take him in her arms and offer comfort as one might to a child but was afraid of rejection so she sat, silent, unable to stop the tears spilling over and sliding down her cheeks. She sniffed, groped for a hanky, then failing to find one put up her hand and brushed her cheeks with her fingers.

The gesture caught Mark's attention. He looked at her in surprise. 'Why the tears?' he asked. 'You're not — no, you couldn't be

— not crying for me, are you?'

Clare nodded, not trusting herself to speak. 'Oh, Mark, how dreadful for you. I feel quite ashamed. I've been telling you my pathetic little story and all the time you had this real big hurt'

'But Clare, didn't you understand why I was telling you? I hadn't really finished — I was going to say you had brought me back to life — emotionally, I mean. You mustn't cry for me. It will always be there the pain and the guilt — but I can put it where it belongs now. Behind me. That was what I wanted to tell you — you've woken me up somehow. I can feel again, I can dare to love again. I thought you realized that.'

Clare shook her head. 'Not really. I thought you had just thought up this marriage idea so that we could both get what we wanted.'

'So I did, I admit that. I didn't bargain for the fact that I might discover that what I wanted more than anything was you!'

'I guess I felt the same. I wanted that house. When I say it was my dream house, I mean that quite literally. I have dreamed about it. I think I must have remembered it from that childhood visit. I wish I had some memory of Hester too.' Clare screwed up her face, trying to remember, and Mark laughed.

'One of the things I love about you, Clare

Davenport, is the way you can look like the sophisticated city lawyer and act like a gamine child.'

She stared at him, not sure whether to be offended, then one word stood out like a blazing light. He had said that he loved her.

'Can you stop staring at me in what I can only describe as a totally spaced-out manner and revert to hot-shot lawyer for a moment. Do you think our friend Robert is likely to act on his threats?'

She shook her head. 'I honestly don't know. The last couple of months have taught me that I don't really know him very well; at least not as well as I thought I did.'

Mark shrugged. 'Well, if he does we'll just have to let Timothy sort him out. After all, he was the instigator of all this. He made the will.'

'At Hestor's bidding,' Clare reminded him. 'And there is nothing she can do to help us now.'

'I wouldn't be too sure. She was a powerful organizer. I can't believe she isn't still at it in some other dimension. Bizarre her will may have been but it achieved what she wanted; her only living blood relation inheriting and forcing me to pick up the pieces of my life and learn to live — and love — again.'

There it was again. 'You have said that

word twice now,' Clare pointed out.

'And which word would that be? Let me think — it wouldn't be 'love', would it?'

'You did know what you were saying, I suppose?'

'I knew. I didn't know if you had heard — and what your response would be.'

'I heard — and this is my response . . . ' Clare reached her hand across the breakfast bar and caught his. Holding it tight, she pulled herself up on her stool, leaned over the breakfast dishes and kissed him softly on the lips.

'How do you feel about staying married?' he asked.

'Good, real good!' she told him.